# MY FAIR VERONA

## CHEY CARNER

CARNER HOUSE PUBLISHING

*For my sister, Kathy, who has always inspired and encouraged a love of reading.*

*&*

*For my husband, who has always supported my dreams.*

# CHAPTER ONE

The clock on the wall chimed, ringing through the empty office like a warning on the air. One. Two. Three. Four. Five. Then finally, one last chime. *Six already? I'm going to be late for dinner again.* Adam thought as he snapped closed the massive law book he had spent the last three hours reading. He massaged his temples with a groan before gathering his briefcase and straightening his tie. Adam looked back at the book and thought about taking it with him, but pushed the thought away as he headed for the door. Adam noticed his reflection as he passed the mirror that hung in the lobby. His dark hair was slightly tousled, and the stubble on his jaw prominent. Even on his light brown skin, the five o'clock shadow aged him by about five years. *Christ, I look like I haven't slept for weeks,* he thought, as he turned away from the mirror. He was just locking the door when his phone lit up, indicating a text message. Adam smiled as he read the text from his wife and sent his reply. Three letters. "OMW."

The commute from Bowen and Gray, the law office where Adam worked, to his house took about twenty minutes. He worked in the city, but his home was in Ross Lake, Iowa's tiny town on a big lake; that was how the locals described it. There wasn't much to do in Ross Lake, but it had some of the most beautiful views. The hillside by the lake, or 'The Bluff' if you were local, was a great place to picnic in the summer, and it was also a trendy make-out spot for teenagers. Adam and his high school sweetheart had spent many date nights there in his car, overlooking the starry sky reflected on the surface of the water.

When Adam reached the front door of his house, his wife, Verona, greeted him wearing the tiny negligee that she had worn on their wedding night three years ago. His eyes brightened at the sight of her standing in the doorway. Adam couldn't help but smile. She handed him one of the glasses of wine she was holding as she moved back so Adam could enter and close the door.

"What's the occasion?" Adam asked as he took the glass that she offered him and planted a tender kiss on her lips.

"I thought we should celebrate. I got a job!" She sipped her wine as she waited for her husband to inquire further.

"Well, are you going to tell me about it or keep me in suspense?" He teased. He moved toward her, wrapping his free hand around her waist and holding her close to him.

"You're looking at the receptionist for Dr. Grant Hudson-Psychiatrist. The job comes with medical, dental, vision, not to mention it's a huge pay increase from the clinic." Verona barely had time to set down her glass of wine before Adam swept her off her feet and into a celebratory hug. Adam was much taller than his wife, so when she pulled him into a passionate kiss, he was still holding her up off the floor, and he didn't put her down until they reached the bed.

That seemed so long ago. Now, Adam was thirty-four, and he and Verona had been married for fifteen years. Those memories of the happy times had come flooding back recently, too little, too late, since Adam had not seen or heard from his wife in three days. Admittedly, their relationship had become strained over the last couple of years, with both of them working long hours.

The caseloads at Bowen and Gray seemed to be continuously growing in both numbers and difficulty. Many nights, Adam would come home so late that Verona was fast asleep in their bed. He would crawl in beside her, and they would sleep back to back without touching. Other nights, Adam would come home early, hoping to surprise her, only to find that she wasn't there. He would message her to ask where she was, and sometimes, she would reply; *Sorry, Girl's Night* or *Spa Weekend Retreat.* She seemed to have this whole other life that did not include Adam.

He supposed it was fair because what did he expect her to do, sit at home all the time waiting for him? These are things that Adam had accepted at the time. He thought that if he let her indulge in these whims and have this life outside of their marriage, that his focus could be on work and saving money for their future, a time when he envisioned them retiring from their jobs and traveling the world together.

Adam was now at the Ross Lake Police Department, sitting across the desk from a husky police officer with gray hair and a mustache, describing the last time he saw his wife. One of the fluorescent lights above buzzed and flickered just enough to be distracting as Adam tried to think.

"She was sleeping when I left for work." He told the officer.

"And when you came home, she was just gone?" The officer scribbled something on a yellow legal pad as he listened.

"It's not that she was gone, I had come home plenty of times, and she wasn't there, but she won't answer her cell, and she has been gone for three days now. Workdays at that. Doctor Hudson called me, worried because she hasn't shown up for work either. The strangest part is that her car is still in our driveway."

"Mm-hmm." The officer mumbled as he continued to write. Adam glanced at his desk for a name plaque, but there wasn't one. He looked at the officer's uniform shirt and spotted the silver tag with his last name on it. Officer Dunn cleared his throat before continuing.

"How would you describe your relationship?" He asked, looking up from his notes for the first time. There it was- the dreaded question. *He's going to say she left on her own and doesn't want me to find her.* Adam thought.

"Were things good, or had you been fighting?" Officer Dunn clarified, sensing Adam's pause. Adam didn't want to answer, he didn't know how this could be important or help find his wife, but he knew that it would make him look guilty if he didn't answer.

"We hadn't been fighting more than usual, but I also wouldn't say things had been good, not for a while, for a few years at least. Disappearing isn't Verona's style though, she would have just told me to pack my stuff and move out, or she'd have gone to her sister's house. She was headstrong like that and always knew what she wanted." Tears started welling up in Adam's eyes, and he looked away from Officer Dunn long enough to wipe them. When he looked back at the officer, Adam noticed that his demeanor had softened.

"Have you contacted her family, friends, and co-workers?" Officer Dunn asked.

"Of course, everyone I could think of."

"Okay, we will need access to her bank accounts, credit cards, and cell phone. We will track all of these things and see what we turn up. Did you happen to bring in a recent photo of her?" He asked.

Adam handed over the most recent photo he had. It was one that she had posted to her social media account while hiking the north face of Alyeska on her office trip to Alaska. She had been gone for a month and had only been back for a couple of months before Adam came home to find her gone again. Officer Dunn took the photo, studied it, and then picked up the phone. He pressed three numbers and said;

"I have a missing person report. okay, I will send him over." He hung up the phone and gathered his notes and the photo of Verona.

"Take this over to that window, and they will get some fliers made for you." Officer Dunn patted Adam's shoulder. "We'll do everything we can to find her." He said with a reassuring nod.

Adam walked glumly to the window as if in a hazy, dreamlike state, still not sure if this was happening or if at any moment he would awaken from this nightmare to find his wife asleep beside him. The rest of the day was a blur. Adam walked all over town, posting the missing person flier on every notice board or telephone pole in the city. When he got down to his last copy, he stopped at his house to make more.

Adam walked into the house and looked around. It felt so empty. He immediately fell to the floor, sobbing like a child who had just crashed their bike. *I'm so sorry, Verona. Really, so fucking sorry. Please just come home.* He laid on the floor in the fetal position, unable to sleep and unable to muster the motivation to pull himself up off the floor. He laid there just thinking of all the ways he could have been a better husband, and suddenly the good memories that filled his thoughts over the last few days turned into every argument that they had in just the last four years alone.

They started out fighting over having children. Verona had always wanted children; Adam didn't. He had been focused on his career, which was taking off, and wanted to wait until he felt comfortable enough not to work as much. Adam had finally relented in the end, and they had tried to have a baby. When it didn't happen, they fought about who was at fault. Verona had begged him to "get checked," and he had refused. It was an invasion of privacy the way he saw it. Verona had gone to a fertility doctor independently and found out that nothing was preventing her from reproducing.

When Adam refused to get checked himself, she had started in again about him not wanting children. It wasn't too long after that their arguments turned into silence for days on end. Adam would try to talk to his wife about whatever they disagreed on, and she wouldn't even state her case anymore; she didn't even try to change his mind. What Adam saw was pure apathy. Maybe it was because she didn't feel there was anything left to fight for; their love had died.

Adam recalled one fight, in particular, it had been after his second year at Bowen and Gray. He had been on a complicated case that his firm had just lost, and he had not come home that night. Instead, Adam had fallen asleep at his desk while searching for a precedent that could overturn their client's sentence. Verona had made a lovely dinner and set the table with their wedding china in an attempt to cheer him up. Adam had told her that afternoon that he would see her for dinner, but he lost track of time and worked until he was too exhausted to hold his eyes open anymore.

Hours later, Adam woke up with ink stains on his cheek from the fountain pen that he had used to scribble his notes. When he got home, his dinner was still on the table, cold and unappetizing. She hadn't even put it away. There was a note on the table that read; *I'm at my sister's. Don't call.*

It had taken everything in him not to go over there and explain; he tried to dial her number but changed his mind just before hitting 'call' and pressed the home button instead. She stayed gone for two days then. On the third day, he went to Verona's sister's place.

When Milan opened the door, she rolled her eyes and tried to close it again, but Adam stopped it with his foot.

"Please, I just need to talk to my wife." He said.

Milan studied his face; he hadn't shaved or slept in days.

"You look like shit. Are you drunk?" She asked, scowling at him. Adam stared at her in shock.

"Of course not, I'm distraught. My wife hasn't come home in three days." He argued, maybe a little too defensively. "Now, may I speak with her, please?" He asked as politely as he could muster while removing his foot from the door.

"You could," Milan said. "If she were here, but she isn't."

"That's right; It's Monday. She must be at work." Adam hurried away, leaving Milan standing in the doorway, watching him go.

When he walked into the office building, he headed straight to the elevator and hit the third-floor button. *Who puts a shrink's office three floors up?* Adam thought as the elevator lurched upward. When the doors opened to the third floor, Adam ran out and headed left down the hall to suite 326. When he saw his wife sitting behind the desk, talking to a patient on the phone, his heart jumped into his throat. He hadn't precisely thought out what he would say to her, but the expression on her face when their eyes met told him to tread carefully.

They went to lunch that day, and he explained and apologized. He begged her to come home, and she did, but things weren't the same. Verona no longer waited for him or expected anything from him. In some ways, he felt like she was accepting that his job was essential and was filling her life with things that made her happy, but another part of him knew that those things no longer included him. Adam thought about just letting her go, asking her if a divorce would make her happy, but he wasn't ready to lose her. Thinking back on it now, he realized how selfish he had been. *She deserved better than me,* he thought.

Now, alone on the floor, curled in the fetal position, Adam felt like she was gone for good this time, and it was killing him. He imagined her on a beach somewhere, in that blue halter bikini that she looked so beautiful wearing. He saw her clearly, sipping pina colada from half a coconut shell, living her best life, free of him and their toxic marriage. He cried until he had no tears left.

# CHAPTER TWO

It had been three weeks since Adam filed the missing person report when a couple of hikers happened upon a woman's body in the woods. The recent rainfall caused a mudslide and the loose dirt that concealed the corpse ran downhill, revealing the crime.

Officer Harold Dunn, and his partner, Sara Jensen, secured the area and preserved as much of the scene as possible while waiting for a forensics team to extract the body. Officer Jensen was a fresh-faced rookie, straight out of the academy. She had never seen a dead body, other than the corpse they had to examine for her criminal justice class. That body had already been embalmed and dissected, though. She fought the urge to throw up as the stench of decomposition wafted in her direction.

"Go take the witness statements, Jensen," Dunn told her, more as mercy than a delegation of a menial task. She quickly obliged and headed back behind the police tape to talk to the hikers. When the medical examiner and forensic investigators arrived, Officer Dunn led them to the body. He watched them place little yellow placards down as they photographed evidence-something he had already done, but he guessed they needed to make sure no one moved anything or contaminated the scene. After about an hour, they began to exhume the body. Even in her current state of decomposition, Officer Dunn recognized the long auburn hair, and high cheekbones from the photograph Adam Sheffield had given him.

"Her features match the description of a missing person case I got a few weeks ago," Dunn remarked. "I'll call the husband to see if he can meet us at the morgue to ID." He walked off back behind the tape and pulled out his phone.

"Hi, Yes, this is officer Dunn calling. I wish I had better news for you. We found a body matching your wife's description. We should have her at the medical examiner's office in about an hour. Would you have time to stop by to ID? Great. I will call you when we finish up here, and you can meet us there."

Dunn started the recorder on his phone and headed back to the crime scene, changing his gloves before stepping through the tape. The investigators had already placed the body in a body bag and were about to zip it up when Dunn stopped them.

"Mind if I take a look? He asked, holding up his gloved hands to show that he was following protocol. They stepped aside and let him look over the body. "Female, in her early thirties, about a hundred and forty pounds. She looks to be about 5'7" with auburn hair." He lifted one of her eyelids with his gloved fingertip. "Blue eyes... Hmm." As Officer Dunn held her left hand up to examine her fingernails, he noticed something else. "No wedding rings." Officer Dunn placed her arm gently back inside the bag and stepped back so they could zip her up. Dunn removed his gloves and pulled his phone out of his pocket to stop the recording.

After the medical examiners loaded the woman into the ambulance, and the investigators had collected every fiber and lifted every print from the area, Officer Dunn and Officer Jensen cleaned up and removed the tape. Dunn looked at Jensen. "You okay, rookie?" he asked, with genuine concern on his face.

"I'm fine." She replied. "I mean, it's a little scary. That woman is around my age." Jensen shrugged, but Dunn knew that she was thinking about how easily something could happen to her. They head back to the cruiser in silence and Dunn drove them to the medical examiner's office. By the time they arrived, the coroner already had the body cleaned up and presentable.

"Wow, You work fast," Dunn commented. "You have a cause of death already?" Dunn was surprised at the young coroner's speed and efficiency.

"It wasn't hard. There was a struggle before your victim died. She has contusions around her throat like someone grabbed her by the neck, Not too hard, but just hard enough to leave bruises. The main cause of death was blunt force trauma to the back of the head. Lividity indicates she was struck from behind and fell forward, but then was buried face-up after death, about an hour or two, which is about how long it might take to dig a hole, but that last part is pure speculation." The medical examiner looked proud of himself.

"Thank you, Mr. Kingston. That's most helpful." Dunn turned to leave, already thinking about the scenarios in which a person being choked, could be hit from behind hard enough to cause their death. His mind went straight to cheating and someone catching them in the act. If that were the case, there would be either two witnesses or two victims.

"There's one more thing," Kingston called out to Dunn. "She was three months pregnant, give or take a week or two."

"Shit... I wonder if her husband knew?" Dunn walked out, still thinking to himself. *If Adam Sheffield knew his wife was pregnant, he would have mentioned it, unless he didn't know, or if he thought that knowing would make him look guilty.* Dunn rushed back into the morgue.

"Get me a DNA workup on the fetus. I want to know who the father is and keep this between us for now." He walked back out, gears still turning in his mind. He rounded the corner and crashed into Adam, who was turning down the hall at the same time.

"I'm sorry, are you okay?" Dunn asked the ghost-faced man he saw before him. Adam nodded; he looked as if he could vomit at any moment. Dunn would almost not have recognized him if he saw him out on the street. Adam had lost a good thirty pounds and hadn't shaved in weeks. His clothes smelled like he had been wearing the same outfit for days and spilling whiskey on them for just as long.

"I'm here to..." His voice caught in his throat, and he couldn't even choke out the words, but Dunn nodded and led him into the room where the body was still on the table covered with a white sheet. Adam walked up to the foot of the table. The tag on her toe read; Doe, Jane. The medical examiner pulled the sheet back off her face, and Adam broke into tears. He reached for her face, which was cold and bluish-gray. *God fucking damn it!* Adam screamed in his head as he slammed his fist on the exam table that held his wife and cried.

Adam lifted his tear-streaked face to look at Mr. Kingston. "It's her. Verona Sheffield" He pulled himself away from her body as Mr. Kingston covered Verona's face once more.

"Mr. Sheffield, I know this is a difficult time for you, but since foul play is suspected, we need to investigate all possible suspects. As her husband, I can't rule you out until I have investigated Thoroughly. Will you consent to a search of your home and vehicle, Mr. Sheffield?" Dunn looked at him calmly.

"Someone murdered my wife, and you want to search my home?" Adam shouted. "Why don't you go out and find her murderer instead of wasting time accusing me of killing my wife? You can conduct a search of my home when you have a warrant. Now, if you will excuse me, I have to inform my wife's family and begin her funeral arrangements." Adam was fuming as he pushed past Officer Dunn and walked quickly from the morgue. Jensen came up behind her partner and clapped his shoulder in a strange attempt at comforting him.

"It's okay. Anger is part of the grieving process. He will come around." She told him. Dunn looked at his watch.

"Shit, it's after five. We aren't getting a warrant until Monday at least. How about we grab dinner, and then we will try to tail Adam for a bit in the unmarked. We will see if he gives anything away or acts suspicious." Jensen nodded in response, and they headed out.

"We need to think about motive. What motive could a husband have to kill his wife?" Dunn asked once they were in the car. Jensen looked at him, thoughtfully.

"Maybe she was unfaithful, Maybe she was going to leave him, or both. He might have had a sizable life insurance policy on her." Jensen brainstormed out loud.

"That's easy enough to check. We can start there." Dunn said.

"How could we find out the other things?" Jensen asked.

"Once we get her phone records released, we will be able to see every call she made, and every text she sent, even the deleted stuff," Dunn told her.

"What about the location of her phone? No one ever found it, and she never set up 'find my phone.' Where ever her phone is, it might be where the killer is too." Jensen said. Dunn had never thought of that; he honestly hadn't given much thought to Verona's missing phone at all.

"You're a genius. Maybe we will find Verona's phone when we look through Adam's place on Monday."

Dunn and Jensen ordered some food from a fast food place on the way and ate in the car. Adam was at Verona's sister's house when Dunn and Jensen located him. Dunn parked the unmarked vehicle up the street so Adam wouldn't notice them. They watched the house for quite a while before Adam finally opened the door. He wrapped Milan in a tight hug, and Dunn could tell from their body language that they had both been crying. For a while, Adam sat in his car, and Dunn noticed him banging his fists on the steering wheel.

"His emotions seem to be spot on for a guy who just found out his wife was murdered," Dunn muttered aloud.

"I agree. It seems like Adam cared for her and is shocked by her death. Someone capable of killing their wife would likely only act like this if they knew they were being watched." Dunn looked over at Jensen, who looked like she was about to cry. He tried to think of something comforting yet insightful to say, but before he could think of something, they heard Adam's engine roar to life.

"Let's go," Dunn said as he waited for Adam to get a head start before pulling out behind him.

They followed far enough behind to avoid detection, and Adam's next stop was Verona and Milan's Parents' place.

"This is Madeline and Henry Warren's place, the victim's parents," Dunn explained.

"Wait, Madeline Warren... The Madeline Warren? As in the artist?" Jensen looked shocked.

"I take it you're familiar with her work?" Dunn chuckled a little.

"When I went to college, I minored in contemporary art. She was the focus of the entire class, her work, her technique, she's amazing. I can't believe it; please tell me we will get to interview her?" Jensen asked, hopefully.

"I imagine we will at some point, but we have to remain professional." Dunn gave her a sideways glance that made her realize that she sounded like a fangirl or a groupie for the time's biggest rock band.

"Sorry, yes, of course." She said, trying hard to contain the excitement on her face.

Adam spent a lot less time with the Warrens than he did with Milan. After twenty minutes, Adam returned to his car, leaving Mrs. Warren sobbing into her husband's shoulder. Just then, Dunn's text notification went off.

"DNA results from the M.E. We should head back; besides, something tells me they could use a little time to process." Dunn started the car and pulled away from the curb, turning down the next street so they could avoid Adam seeing them. They continue the ride back to the morgue in silence, contemplating the results of the stakeout, or perhaps the results of the DNA test.

With the results of the DNA test back, Dunn called Judge Cross on his home phone to ask for an emergency warrant.

"We need to collect DNA evidence, your honor, and Mr. Sheffield would not consent to a search, I would like to get over there before he has time to dispose of any evidence." Dunn listened and wrote down a number on his notepad. "Yes, your honor. Thank you. Sorry to bother you at home. Bye." Jensen looked hopeful.

"So, did we get the warrant?" She asked.

"Yes. He's going into the office now to sign it. It will be ready in thirty minutes. Assemble a team of investigators to take with us while I go pick it up." Jensen nods and hurried off as Dunn headed for the door.

An hour later, they knocked on Adam's door to serve the warrant. Adam stayed out of the way as the team entered and began combing through his belongings, his wife's belongings, and all the intimate details of their life together. Adam sat on the porch swing with his elbows on his knees and his head in his hands. He watched the "evidence" being bagged and tagged and placed into a white banker's box.

"What is all of this stuff? It can't possibly be important because I didn't murder my wife." Adam objected loudly to Officer Dunn as they carried the banker box to the back of the police car.

"I'm sorry, Mr. Sheffield, it's just procedure," Dunn said as he closed the door. "We're all done here for now. Thank you for your time." Dunn turned back to his vehicle.

"Not like I had a choice," Adam muttered as he stomped back to his front porch, watching them drive away.

Dunn pulled the blue toothbrush from the evidence box back at the station and removed it from the evidence bag. He placed it with the DNA results of the baby and headed for the lab.

"Can you pretty please run this DNA to see if they match? And if it isn't too much trouble, rush the results?" Dunn asked.

"Of course, Officer Dunn." The lab tech took the sample and placed it at the front of the waitlist. "It will be about an hour. I have something in the machine right now, and I can't stop it in the middle of the analysis." Dunn nodded and thanked her again. He headed back to his desk and began looking through the evidence box. Dunn put on gloves and then pulled out a small photo album. He turned the pages, noticing that this album was all pictures from Verona's Alaska trip. Adam said that it was an office trip, but Verona and a gentleman in his late thirties were the only people in the photos.

Dr. Hudson? Dunn wondered? The first photo was of Verona pretending to drink from a chocolate fountain; the next was a photo of her ice skating on a frozen pond behind a beautiful hotel. Dunn turned the page. A picture of Verona raising a glass in a toast caught his eye. *No wedding rings.* Dunn turned to the next photograph. It was Verona holding up a menu at a fancy restaurant. Jack Sprat. That was the name of the place. As he flipped through the album, Dunn looked for Verona's rings in each one. She didn't wear her rings the entire trip. It doesn't mean anything though, maybe she just never wears them.

Dunn Picked up another photo out of the box. This one was in a frame. Verona and Adam stood together, smiling, and her left hand was posed lovingly on his chest, displaying her white gold wedding band and princess-cut diamond engagement ring. *Happier times, huh?* Dunn thought as he placed the picture back into the box.

"Ready to head over to The Warren's place?" Jensen startled him and made him drop the picture, rather than gently placing it back in the box.

"Sure," Dunn said.

They drove back to The Warren's place in silence, knowing that a hard conversation lay ahead. When they arrived, Mrs. Warren invited them in. Her eyes were red from crying, and a pile of used tissues filled the small garbage can beside her recliner. She had a book, open to the page she had been trying to read, placed face-down on the end table to hold her page. Mrs. Warren had decorated her home lavishly with sculptures and paintings, all no doubt, Warren originals. The room they sat in now, Mrs. Warren had called 'the parlor'. The furniture was all black and white, and the style was contemporary. A white grand piano sat in the back corner, and a small library with reading benches next to bay windows dominated the front of the room.

"You have a beautiful home, Mrs. Warren," Jensen said.

"Thank you, dear.." She said with a sniffle as she took another tissue from the box on the end table. Mr. Warren entered the room and sat down on the sofa next to his wife. He took her hands in his.

"How can we help you, officers?" Henry Warren asked.

"We just had a few questions to ask you about your daughter. We will try to be brief." Dunn began. Henry and Madeline nodded.

"Can you think of anyone who might want to harm your daughter?" Dunn asked. Henry squirmed in his seat a little and cleared his throat.

"No, She was kind, kept to herself too." He told them.

"What was her relationship like with her husband, Adam?"

"They fought a lot but always seemed to work it out. She was stubborn and headstrong, he is very focused on his career, but he's a good man. I don't think he would ever harm her." Madeline said as she fought back the tears again.

"Besides Adam, who did Verona spend the most time with?" Jensen asked as she crossed that question off her list.

Henry and Madeline looked at each other. Henry looked a little nervous, and Madeline was on the verge of tears again.

"She spent a lot of time with Dr. Hudson. That psychiatrist she works for. They just got back from Alaska a few weeks before..." Madeline's voice trailed off, but Jensen knew that she meant before Verona went missing.

"If you can think of anything else, please let us know," Dunn said, handing his card to Henry. Dunn and Jensen showed themselves out.

"We're almost off duty for today. Tomorrow, I say we pay a visit to Dr. Hudson." Dunn suggested.

"Sounds good to me. Wanna grab dinner?" Jensen asked.

They spent the rest of the evening talking about anything and everything -except work. No thoughts of dead bodies or suspects invaded their dinner. They weren't officers Dunn and Jensen; they were Harry, and Sara, two friends enjoying a meal. The separation was necessary, at least for Sara. Tomorrow would be another day, and more heartbreaking discussions about Verona, a girl no older than she was.

# CHAPTER THREE

The office of Dr. Grant Hudson was closed. Officer Dunn looked at his watch. It was eleven in the morning on a business day. The hours posted on the door said M-F 8 to 4. Dunn called the number only to get an immediate answering machine with a female's voice.

"Hi, you have reached the office of Dr. Grant Hudson. If you are having suicidal thoughts or this is an emergency, please hang up and call 9-1-1. To schedule an appointment..." Dunn hung up. *It looks like I will have to make a house call. I have to find out where he lives.* Dunn got back into his cruiser and drove to the station. He put a tech on the task of pulling up Dr. Hudson's home address from his DMV records.

"Hey, Rookie! Glad you're here!" He called out to Jensen as she entered the office. "I'm about to head over to Dr. Hudson's place to talk to him. You coming?" He asked as he gathered his things. Jensen nodded and followed after Dunn's quickened pace.

"What's the rush?" She asked as she struggled to keep up.

"Well, it's normal business hours, and his office is closed. It seems strange right after someone murdered his secretary, doesn't it?" Dunn asked.

"Not really, if you think about it. I mean, Verona and Dr. Hudson worked together in a small office; he probably knew her pretty well and is grieving." Jensen suggested.

"Well, we will ask him when we get there." Dunn started the car and whipped it out of the parking lot.

They arrived at Dr. Hudson's home address by noon. It was out in the country, tucked away behind an apple orchard. He had horses grazing in the field behind a wooden fence running the length of the long driveway. Dunn knocked loudly on the front door and waited about two seconds before impatiently ringing the doorbell five times in quick succession. Finally, there was a shuffle from the other side of the door.

"Who's banging on my door like the po-" Grant swung the door open "-lice." He finished as Dunn and Jensen held up their badges.

Standing before Officers Dunn and Jensen was a scruffy, half-dressed man; the flecks of gray in his dark hair were highlighted by the midday sun, and he smelled strongly of whiskey and body odor, indicative of a three-day bender at least.

"Sorry to bother you at home Doctor Hudson but we had some questions about your secretary. May we come in?" Officer Jensen took the lead. Her voice tended to have a calming effect. Jensen gestured to the foyer as she waited for Grant to answer. Finally, he moved to the side, extending his arm with the door wide open. Once Dunn and Jensen were inside, Grant closed the door and led them to a sitting room to the foyer's left.

"Would you care for a drink?" Grant asked as he moved to the bar. Empty whiskey bottles and dirty glasses covered the length of the bar, but Dr. Hudson took no notice as he poured himself a drink.

"I'm afraid we can't; we're on the clock," Jensen said with a tap of her watch.

"More for me then." Grant pours even more into his glass, ignoring the two-finger rule and filling it up with whiskey. He set his glass on the coffee table and flopped back on the couch with exasperation.

"So, what questions do you have for me?" Grant ran his fingers through his hair, and Jensen caught herself thinking about how handsome he would be if he were cleaned up and didn't smell of alcohol. He had a slight British accent that made him seem exotic, but his accent wasn't as thick as most, meaning he had spent a great deal of time in America.

"I am sure you have already heard that the body of your secretary, Verona Sheffield, was found."

"Verona Warren-Sheffield." Grant corrected.

"Yes, well, we are investigating her death, and it would help us if you could give us any information about her. Like, did you ever see her arguing with anyone?" Jensen asked as she positioned a notepad and pen to take notes.

"You mean besides her neglectful husband?" There was a bitterness in his voice at the word husband.

"Sure, had they ever argued at the office?" Jensen looked up at Grant as he thought.

"One time she came in stressed out, she looked like she had slept in her clothes, and he came in a couple of hours later and made a scene. She went to lunch with him so they could talk privately. I guess it all worked out because things returned to normal the next day."

"What was your relationship with her? From the evidence we collected from her house and social media, we know that you guys spend a lot of time together both in the office and out."

Grant looked shocked. "Am I a suspect? Do I need a lawyer?"

"Doctor Hudson, we are just trying to gather all the information we can. You never know what piece of evidence will be the key to cracking the case." Jensen reassured. Grant nodded. "Well, to be completely candid, I fell in love with her. Our relationship began the same as most boss-employee relationships, professional and brief. One night, when she was upset about her husband forgetting their anniversary, he'd claimed that he had to work late, I took her out on our first date. I told her she shouldn't have to spend her anniversary alone. We were friends after that." Grant paused and reached for his drink. He looked at the officers waiting for further questions.

"So, just friends then, or did she reciprocate your feelings?" Jensen asked. She looked at his face and could see from his expression that he was hiding something. "We saw pictures of you two from your office Alaska trip. Are you two the only employees in your office?"

Grant's expression turned hard as stone, and his face reddened. He stood up and moved toward the archway to the foyer. " I am done talking now unless you would like to wait for my lawyer." He pulled his phone out of the pocket of his bathrobe to prove he was serious.

"That won't be necessary right now. Thank you for your time, Dr. Hudson." Dunn and Jensen walked out the front door, and Grant watched as they drove back down the driveway. He returned to his whiskey and took a greedy, angry gulp.

He winced slightly at the burn as the alcohol slid down his throat, then unlocked his phone and started thumbing through the gallery. Tears welled up in his eyes as Grant looked at the photos of Verona. He hovered over the delete button, nearly sobbing.

Grant couldn't bring himself to press it. He threw his phone across the room with all his might. Grant crumpled to his knees as his phone shattered against the wall. After regaining his composure, Grant saw to the wreckage of his cell phone, and much to his surprise, the screen lit up. Even in the phone's shattered state, it still responded to his touch. He dialed his lawyer.

The next morning, Grant, at the behest of his lawyer, walked into the police department clean, sober, and freshly shaven. He asked the dispatcher at the front desk if he could speak with officer Jensen. She smiled and picked up the phone and dialed the extension. At the end of their brief conversation, the receptionist hit a buzzer and directed Grant to Jensen's desk.

"Well, hello there. I didn't expect to see you so soon." Jensen smiled as she nodded toward the empty chair in front of her desk. Grant sat down and cleared his throat before speaking.

"I uh... think we got off on the wrong foot the other day. I know you were doing your job, and I should have been cooperative. That's why I am ready to give my statement." Grant squeezed his hands nervously as Jensen grabbed a pen and a statement form and slid them across the desk in front of him. He picked up the pen and began writing. Just as he finished, Officer Dunn walked over to the desk.

"There's one more thing we need to discuss. If you would, please, follow me." Dunn led Grant to a private interrogation room. The mirror reflected them as they sat down at the table.

"Don't worry; there's no one in there. This information that I am about to give you has to stay between us. This detail of the case is unreleased. Do I have your word?"

Grant nodded eagerly. "Yes."

"Verona was almost four months pregnant when she died. I collected her husband's DNA, and it wasn't a match. Given your romantic relationship with Verona, I am speculating that yours might be. If her husband knew this, that would give him a motive. Would you consent to a DNA test?" Grant put his head in his hands and began sobbing silently. His shoulders heaved and shook with every breath.

"I will give you a few moments to think about it," Dunn said as he stepped out of the room. Dunn stepped into the room on the other side of the two-way mirror and watched as Grant slammed his fist on the table, still crying.

"I don't think it was him." Jensen's voice broke the silence.

"It's usually the spouse; nine times out of ten." Dunn replied.

"So, should we invite him here and tell him the news?" Jensen asked.

"Not yet. For now, let's continue surveillance on Mr. Sheffield, begin surveillance on Dr. Hudson, and in the meantime, we have plenty of other people we can interview. Let's start with her family." Dunn poured a cup of coffee and grabbed a bottle of water from the mini-fridge, then returned to Grant.

"So, have you made a decision?" Dunn offered Grant the water and the coffee. Grant accepted the water, opened it, and drank half in three gulps.

"I'll do it," Grant said.

After Dunn swabbed Grant's mouth and sent the sample off to the lab, Grant sat in his car with everything running through his mind. It was late afternoon now, and there was work to be done. Grant headed back to his house and opened his laptop. He clicked the icon on his desktop for his web browser, and when the search bar came up, he typed; Private investigators near me, and hit search. Immediately, a full page of results appeared, and he scrolled through them.

Grant scrolled past ad after ad until he found what he needed. *This one looks promising, h*e thought to himself as he clicked the link. *Charlotte Bradley, PI. Twelve years of experience, rave reviews. Hundreds of cases solved, personal and corporate work.* When he was satisfied with her credentials, Grant pulled out his busted phone and called Charlotte's listed number.

Charlotte arrived at Grant's house within the hour and approached the door with a muscular man following closely behind her. She was in her forties with sandy blond hair and hazel eyes. When Grant opened the door, he gasped under his breath because she wasn't what he was expecting at all. *It was silly of me to expect someone in a trench coat and a plaid hat.* He laughed at himself a little on the inside, although his sorrow still shined through on the exterior.

"Welcome, please, come in." He moved aside so that both Charlotte and her partner could enter, and he led them to the sitting room.

"Can I offer you a drink, water, tea?" Grant asked.

"No, thank you, dear. Allow me to introduce Kristofer Bradley, my brother, and business partner. There's no need to be nervous. I can tell by your body language, relax and tell us why you have called." Charlotte settled into her seat. "Hold on a moment." She takes a small recorder out of her pocket. "You don't mind if I record, do you?"

"Some of the information I have has not been released to the public, so I would prefer if you didn't." Grant waited for her to switch the recorder back off.

"Very well. Sometimes details you think are unimportant at first can become important later; one good thing about me is I have a fantastic memory. Unfortunately, my memory isn't admissible in court. But I can't record without your permission, so it's off. Whenever you're ready." Grant drew a deep breath and took a moment before beginning.

"For the past two years, I have been having an affair with my married secretary. She was very unhappily married. Her husband was neglectful of her needs, never home, and made her feel unimportant, you know? She talked about leaving him but never found the courage. We were happy, and I loved her. About a month ago now, they found her body. They said it was murder. She was pregnant." Grant choked on his words as the tears fell once more. Charlotte nodded and placed her hand on his shoulder.

"I'm sorry for your loss, even though I know all the kind words won't ease the pain. What will at least bring you closure is finding the one responsible for her murder. Yes?" Grant nodded as he wiped his eyes.

"Was the baby yours?" Charlotte lowered her voice to ask this and bowed her head to meet Grant's eyes.

"I don't know. I gave the police my sample, but the results aren't back yet. If it was..." His words got tangled in a whimper and suffocated` under pressure.

"I'm

taking your case, Dr. Hudson. I will do my best to find out the

truth." Charlotte vowed.

# CHAPTER FOUR

Dunn and Jensen rang the doorbell of Milan Warren's townhouse, and in response, a small dog began yapping on the other side. Finally, Dunn heard heels clicking down the hallway toward the door. Milan opened it with the little dog tucked protectively in her arm.

"Hi, Milan Warren?" Dunn asked. Milan nodded.

"Do you have news about my sister's case?" She asked, hopefully.

"Not yet; we are still investigating. Do you have a few minutes to talk?"

Of course, come in." She told them.

They sat in the living room, and Dunn watched Milan as she sat down, trying her best to be calm. Milan waited for their questions.

"Verona and Milan. You and your sister were both named after Italian cities. Is that where your family is from?" Dunn asked.

"No, it's just our mother's favorite place in the world. A lot of her paintings are from the time she spent admiring the Italian scenery." Milan gestured to an oil on canvas painting above her fireplace of the Milan skyline.

"Was it just you and your sister, or did you have any other siblings?"

"Our brother Roman passed away when he was seventeen. Car crash."

"I'm sorry." Dunn shifted in his chair. "So you and your sister must have been close." It was more of a comment than a question, but Milan responded anyway.

"We weren't as close as I would have liked, knowing now how little time we had. Verona crashed here whenever she was mad at Adam, but usually, we would binge-watch Netflix and eat pints of ice cream while she vented."

Dunn noticed Milan's stone face. Both Adam and Dr. Hudson were devastated by Verona's death, and talking about her stirred their emotions. He thought to himself. Still, he continued, watching her expressions, or lack thereof.

"So Roman was the oldest, you were the middle child, and Verona was the youngest?" Dunn asked as he looked around the room at the family portraits that hung on the wall.

"That's right," Milan replied, following his gaze.

Jensen stood up and took a closer look at the photograph. She gave Dunn a look that told him to keep Milan's attention as she continued looking at things around the room.

"When you found out that your sister was murdered, who was the first person who crossed your mind?" Dunn asked.

"Honestly, Adam. But only because in all the movies, it's always the jealous husband, but Adam would never hurt her. Physically at least. They had been together since high school and married right after; as soon as Verona turned eighteen. He never even raised a hand to her. She would have told me if he had."

"Milan, did your sister have any enemies?" Dunn attempted to shift the conversation to other suspects.

"None that I know about," Milan told him.

"Who were her friends? Adam mentioned that she frequented spa retreats and went out often for girls' nights; any idea who she was with on these occasions?" Dunn pulled out a notepad and got ready to take down names.

"The only mutual friend we have is Stacy Morris; she used to stay over all the time when we were young. She and Verona were pretty good friends until about sophomore year. I used to be good friends with her, but we haven't seen each other for years. I can't say if Verona kept in touch. Other than that, your guess is as good as mine. You can learn a lot from someone's Social page, though." Milan pulled out her phone and opened up the Social app. In seconds she had her sister's profile pulled up with a list of all her friends.

"You can filter her friends by location so you can see only people here in town."

"Thank you, that is very helpful."

"Your sister had been to Alaska recently, right? Do you know anything about that trip?"

"Just that her boss took her for a mental health seminar that was happening in Anchorage. He paid for the whole trip, her room, flight, food, entertainment, and everything. She was pretty lucky to land the job as his receptionist. My boss never even bought me lunch." She chuckled. *The first hint of emotion, and it wasn't sadness.* Strange. Dunn thought.

"Thank you for your time; we won't keep you any longer. If you think of anything that might help us, give me a call, would ya?" He handed her his card with his name, badge number, phone number, and extension to his desk phone.

"I will." Milan led them out and closed the door behind them.


Dunn and Jensen got back in the car and drove around the block. Dunn parked on a cross street that faced Milan's house.

"Notice anything interesting while you were looking around?" Dunn asked.

"She likes to keep things tidy. There wasn't a speck of dust on anything. If she were the cause of blunt force trauma, something tells me she would be the one traumatized." Jensen looked over at Dunn.

"What are you thinking?"

"Just that she seemed oddly undisturbed for someone who Just found out that someone murdered their sister." Dunn watched Milan's door suspiciously.

"I'm fairly certain that I detected a hint of jealousy in her voice when I brought up the Alaska trip," Dunn remarked.

"It wasn't a hint; it was subtle like a baseball bat to the face," Jensen said jokingly. They watched her house for the rest of the evening. It was pretty uneventful until Adam's car pulled to a stop in front of her home. He went inside, but the curtains covered the windows, so Dunn and Jensen couldn't see anything going on in there.

"What do we have to do to get a bug? I would love to be a fly on that wall right now." Jensen said, still staring at the front door.

"I am afraid that recording a person's conversations in their own home is a violation of their constitutional rights, and no judge would grant an order for that unless we had probable cause. That cause would have to include evidence of crimes being committed in the home, or that they were planning to commit a future crime." Dunn said.

Jensen's excitement fell. "So, it's just not going to happen, huh?" She asked with a sigh.

"Afraid not," Dunn replied with a smile and a shrug.

A long time passed; they lost track after the first hour, but finally, Adam walked out of Milan's house, hair a mess, and his tie undone. He got in his car and drove away quickly. Dunn and

Jensen shared a suspicious glance. Inside the house, Milan now slept comfortably in her bed, feeling satisfied.

The next morning, Milan got ready for work, sipped some coffee, and grabbed the mail on her way out the door. She looked through the envelopes, shuffling them front to back as she glanced at each one, then tossed the stack into the garbage bin at the end of her driveway.

She drove down the street the same way she did every workday. She didn't even notice when a beat-up blue station wagon pulled away from the curb right after her. When she arrived at work, she walked into the office of Milan Fashion Magazine without noticing the blue station wagon parked in the parking lot.

Her day was a typical day- running the most prominent fashion magazine in the country. Her reporters and writers would pitch their ideas for new articles; she would approve or deny them. The photographers and models would submit hundreds of photos a day, not all of which would make it into the issue. When Adam arrived to ask her to lunch, Milan eagerly accepted.

"Thank GOD you're here!" She said. "I have just been dying to get out of here. I thought that owning a fashion magazine would be glamorous, but I have spent the day bored out of my mind! I cannot smell another perfume sample today, or I swear my head will explode!"

Well, then, lucky you." Adam tried to sound cheerful.

They left the building together and drove to a tiny cafe near the lake. Adam and Milan took a table on the patio. There was a fountain in the middle of the terrace, and all the tables, covered in white tablecloths, seemed to shine in the afternoon sun.

"Ooh, fancy!" Milan smiled. "This wasn't at all what I had in mind when I thought about grabbing a bite for lunch." Milan's eyes were still wandering around the patio. They were seated by a hostess wearing all black except for her apron, tied around her waist with militant precision. The hostess wore pressed black dress pants, perfectly pleated and wrinkle-free. Their waitress followed shortly after, setting down a glass carafe of water that contained a few cucumber slices and a sprig of rosemary. She placed down two short, and stout stemmed glasses and poured the water into each one.

"May I start you off with a beverage?" The waitress looks at Milan first.

"I'm fine with water, thank you."

"Me too," Adam said. The waitress hands them each a menu and a list of the specials of the day.

"I will give you two a moment to look over the menu." She said and turned her attention to the other tables. A man and a woman were seated at the table right behind them, and Adam could hear their waitress going through the same script.

"Look, Milan, the reason I asked you to lunch today is that we need to talk." He lowered his voice to a whisper. "What happened last night can't happen again. With the police investigating Verona's murder, they could be watching all of us. I mean, you might not be a suspect, but I am because I was her husband; how would it look if I kept coming over in the middle of the night? I think we need to cool things down, at least until they find out who killed Verona."

Milan listened without interrupting and took a sip of her water as she carefully turned her words over in her mind before speaking them.

"I have lived in Verona's shadow my whole life. She was the best student, and a model daughter, she never got into trouble or broke the rules, and everyone always loved her. When you asked her out in high school, she knew I liked you first, but you were interested in her, so of course, I told her to go for it, I thought that it might last a few months and then I would get my chance, but that day never came. I poured my heart into my magazine instead, and the outcome, while pretty great, still felt empty compared to the life I could have had with you, so you will have to forgive me for not letting you walk away from me this easily. You talk about how it would look; it looks like grief. I lost my sister, you lost your wife, and from what they say, misery loves company."

The rest of the lunch was pretty quiet. Adam couldn't bring himself to object, and Milan knew that he wouldn't. They were so preoccupied with each other that they didn't notice that the woman at the table behind them was listening to their whole conversation.

Charlotte and Kristofer Bradley had been following Milan the whole day. They followed Milan from her house to her office building. Charlotte parked their rented, blue station wagon in a spot facing the windows of Milan's office. When Adam came to take Milan to lunch, they followed them to the restaurant. Charlotte chose the table right behind Milan and Adam so that she was able to hear their conversation.

She listened as they talked about their relationship, and she picked up on the jealousy in Milan's voice when she spoke of her sister. When Milan and Adam left, Charlotte and Kristofer tried their best to look uninterested as Adam and Milan drove away.

# CHAPTER FIVE

After lunch, Adam went home with Milan's words still echoing in his mind. "She knew I liked you first." She had said. Adam didn't recall this. His memory of high school wasn't the strongest, but he knew for a fact that Milan had never even talked to him except for the time they went to James Alden's party freshman year, and things got dull. James suggested a game of spin the bottle. He had always had a crush on Milan and was hoping to get a kiss from her. James let her spin first, and after three times around the circle, it landed on Adam. Milan crawled forward to him and stroked his cheek as she moved her hand to the back of his head, pulling him into a deep kiss. Her bold move had taken him by surprise, but he didn't resist and kissed her back. "You're a good kisser." She had told him. The way she smiled at him had made him feel uncomfortable, so he thanked her and then excused himself to the bathroom. *They don't need*

*to know that I meant the bathroom at my house.* Adam thought on his way out the front door.

In the next few weeks, Milan started popping up to talk to him all over school. Her brother, Roman, watching out for her like usual, was almost always by her side, and Verona was never far behind them. Adam remembered how gorgeous he thought Verona was. Adam became infatuated with her; every moment they had together was too short. Still, when he navigated those memories, he looked past Verona to Milan, who was usually standing with her arms crossed, scowling, or sitting on the bench with her arms around her knees pouting. She was used to getting everything she wanted, and watching Adam look at Verona that way must have made her feel so hurt. Despite that, he had asked Verona on a date. She declined and told him that she was dating none other than James Alden.

"When did that happen?" Adam asked.

"Milan set us up last week. We have gone out a few times." Verona looked away from Adam, so she didn't have to see his disappointment. Over the next couple of months, Adam and Verona became close friends. Adam wanted Verona in his life and would happily accept whatever relationship she offered, even if it was only friendship. Verona dated James for about a year, and she didn't like seeing Adam alone, so she set him up with her friend Stacy.

The four of them were inseparable until James broke up with Verona. Adam had been there to comfort her, and even though he was dating her friend, couldn't help longing to kiss Verona. She was his best friend, and Adam loved her. Now that Verona was single, there was nothing to keep him from telling her how he felt.

Verona sat on her bed and cried. Adam wrapped his arm around her shoulder and comforted her. He told her what an idiot James was and that anyone stupid enough to break her heart didn't deserve her love or tears. She laughed a little then looked up at him expectantly. The tension thickened, and as they looked into each other's eyes, they didn't even notice the space between them getting smaller until they were kissing.

Their tender moment ended abruptly, as a loud crash in the doorway brought them back to reality. Adam gasped when he looked up to see Milan at the entrance looking at the two of them with surprise and anger in her eyes.

"You don't waste any time, do you Adam, I mean, she's been single a whole five minutes?" Milan had accused. She stormed out and immediately called Stacy and told her what had happened. Adam fumed. "Why did you do that? You had no right; it wasn't your place." Adam yelled.

"My heartbroken sister's bed isn't *your* place, Adam. You are dating Stacy. She's supposed to be *your* friend." Milan pointed her finger at Verona. Milan turned and stomped from the room and left Verona and Adam staring at each other in shame.

Stacy had been willing to stay with Adam and work it out even though he had kissed Verona, but Adam's feelings for

Verona were just too strong, and he told her it wouldn't be fair to keep stringing her along, knowing how he felt about someone else. Milan had been mad at Adam for a long time after that. Stacy had not spoken to Adam or Verona since he broke up with her.

When Adam asked Verona to the Homecoming dance, she had been cautious about responding. She had said she needed time to think about it, and then Verona joked about waiting to see if she got a better offer. Adam had laughed, but a small part of him was afraid that it was right, and he did not doubt that many requests would come her way.

He always felt like he wasn't good enough for Verona Warren, and at any minute, she was going to wise up and realize it too. In all actuality, the time she spent 'thinking about it was spent trying to find her sister a date. It wasn't too hard to find willing participants, but Milan was quite picky. Adam realized now that this must have been because she was still hoping he would ask her instead. When Milan finally accepted a date, Verona excitedly began planning with Adam.

Verona's dress was sparkling crimson, perfectly matched to the details on Adam's black tux. Her corsage was a red rose with baby's breath on a band of black lace elastic.

While they danced, holding each other close, their heartbeats synchronized as Verona rested her head on Adam's shoulder. They should have felt the eyes on them, but they didn't. They were the only two people in the world at that moment until Verona felt a tap on her shoulder.

Can I cut in?" Stacy smiled at her. "I just want to have a long-overdue chat with him; I'll bring him back," she promised.

Reluctantly, Verona moved to the side as Stacy took Adam's hand, and they walked away from Verona, so she could not overhear them. Adam looked back at his date nervously as Stacy moved in close to slow dance with him. He placed his hands high on her waist and tried his best to keep some space between them. He hadn't been paying attention to what Stacy was saying; he added a nod now and again so that she would think he was listening. Finally, as the song ended, Stacy grabbed his face and pressed her lips firmly to his. It caught him off-guard, and before he could break away, he looked up to see Verona rushing off back through the crowd.

"What have you done?" He shot Stacy an angry look as he took chase after Verona. The music had changed the tempo, and the dance floor became too crowded to move through quickly. He pushed his way through the sea of teenagers and finally reached the doors he had seen Verona run through, only to see her crying in the arms of James Alden.

"You guys set this up!" Adam pointed an accusing finger at James's chest as he stood to push Adam back.

"Don't blame me; at least she didn't catch me kissing my ex!"

Adam blacked out at that very moment, so he doesn't remember what happened; he only remembered Verona's scream and seeing James lying on the floor in a pool of blood as the principal and two homecoming chaperons dragged him away while two others checked on James. They had called Adam's parents to pick him up and told him that they would have to discuss his punishment when he returned to school.

Adam tried to call Verona several times that weekend, but she refused to talk to him. Adam heard that he had broken James's nose, and that was where all the blood had come from, but James was otherwise okay. James's parents were furious and pushed for Adam's expulsion. Adam's parents begged the school to give him another chance. Two weeks had passed while the school discussed and decided whether or not to allow Adam to return. Adam had still not been able to talk to Verona, but finally, the principal called and told him he could return to school, as long as he offered a written apology to James. Adam agreed and hand-delivered the letter to James's house.

On Monday, when Adam was finally able to return to school, he walked quickly toward Verona's locker, hoping to catch her and talk things over, but she was standing there beside James. He leaned against the locker next to hers, looking at her like the wolf looked at Red Riding Hood. Adam clenched his fists and walked past quickly, not looking back to see if she even noticed.

When he left homeroom, Verona was waiting for him. She caught his arm as he walked out, and the anger in his eyes melted away when he turned and saw her face. Adam caressed her cheek with the palm of his hand. A tear fell from her eye and rolled down her cheek as she nuzzled into his touch.

"I missed you." She said. Verona looked up at him. "You scared me. I have never seen you so angry. I didn't know what was going to happen..." Her voice trailed off, and Adam just wrapped her in his arms.

"I'm sorry for everything. I don't want you ever to have to feel afraid of me again. I was never upset with you. Stacy and James set me up that night at the dance. They wanted you to see Stacy kissing me so that James could-"

"-I know." She interrupted and pulled his lips to hers.

From that moment on, they didn't leave each other's side.

A knock on Adam's door brought him out of his thoughts and back into the present. He opened it to see Officer Jensen and Officer Dunn with coffee in hand. They held one out to him and looked at him sympathetically.

"Is this a bad time? We just wanted to go over some new information and see if it sparks anything." Jensen said. Adam took the coffee from her and motioned them into the kitchen, where he took a seat at the table. Jensen and Dunn sat across from him.

"So this is going to be hard to hear, but the autopsy revealed that Verona was pregnant. She was about three months along. We thought if you knew that, surely you would have mentioned it." Jensen waited, giving Adam time to process her words. Surprisingly, it wasn't sadness but anger that flashed in Adam's eyes.

"Right after we got married, we tried to start a family. We tried for two years with no success, not even a missed period in two years. Three months before she went missing, she was in Alaska during that time. Verona was in Alaska with Doctor Hudson. I was so stupid. I can't believe I couldn't see it. All the conferences, office trips, maybe even spa weekends and girls' nights." He stood up, clenching his jaw.

"I'm sorry, but I think I need to be alone." He walked toward the door and held it open for the officers. They nodded and left without objection, sharing a glance between them as they descended the steps.

Adam paced the living room floor glancing out the window now and again to make sure the officers had left. Then he drove to Doctor Hudson's office. He sat outside in his car, just watching the building. Several people walked in and out. There were several offices in that building, so there was no way to know where they were going or coming from. Adam had no idea what he would say to Grant Hudson when they came face to face, and as he sat watching the building, every scenario played out in his mind. The most satisfying fantasy was one of his hands around Dr. Hudson's throat, strangling the life out of him. The edges of Adam's vision grew bright white, and everything else became far away as he let the anger overtake him. He got out of the car and walked to the front door and straight to the elevator. He pressed number three, and when the doors opened, he turned left and walked to suite 326.

Adam hadn't been to this office since the day he took Verona to lunch after their fight. Adam imagined walking in and seeing his wife on the phone at her desk. He imagined that look she used to give him when he showed up unannounced. *It all makes so much sense now,* he thought.

It wasn't Verona, but a woman in her sixties, or thereabout. She had gray hair, and she wore bifocals.

"Do you have an appointment?" Adam's vision returned to normal as he realized she was speaking to him, but he hadn't heard what she said, so when he looked at her with apparent confusion, she repeated her question. Adam shook his head.

"No, sorry." He told her.

"Well, I can help you with that. Would you like to make an appointment?"

Adam again shook his head and turned back toward the door when Doctor Hudson came out of his office and spotted him.

"Adam?" Dr. Hudson sounded surprised. Adam paused with his hand on the door handle but then turned back to face the man he had come to see.

"Do you want to talk in my office?" He asked, noting the conflict in Adam's eyes.

Adam followed him into his office and looked around as Dr. Hudson closed the door and directed Adam to the comfortable-looking sofa along the right wall. Then Dr. Hudson sat across from him in a leather armchair. Between them sat a nicely decorated coffee table and a handy place for the box of tissues that sat upon it.

"So I can only guess that you are here to talk about Verona."

"Doctor Hudson, I-" Adam's words caught in his throat like he had eaten a handful of cotton.

"Please, Adam, call me Grant; you're not a patient. We are simply two adults having a conversation." Grant waited for Adam to speak again.

Adam sat silently for quite a while, not sure what to say. He had wanted to scream, Adam had wanted to hurt Grant the way he was hurting, but now, being here in front of him, Adam could see the pain written on his face, and he knew that Grant was heartbroken in the same way.

"I came here because I was angry. I just found out about Verona's pregnancy. The timeline of which puts her in Alaska when the baby would have been..." Adam started to cry. He hated being so vulnerable, and his feelings were mostly of regret for not making the most of what he had while his wife was alive. Grant nodded.

"I can imagine this discovery has made you quite angry with me, and I do not blame you. So you can ask me anything, and I will answer honestly." Grant said.

"How long? How long had you been having an affair with my wife?" Adam could feel the anger rising in him again, but he stifled it down.

Grant thought before he answered because he knew the answer would cause Adam pain, but he had promised to be honest.

"We had been seeing each other for the last two years." Grant tried to keep his voice sympathetic and calm.

"Wow, that long..." Adam was in shock. A million thoughts raced through his mind of the last two years' events and the moments shared between him and Verona. There weren't many. Most of his memories of the previous two years were of him coming in to find dinner long since cleaned up, or no dinner at all, and Verona either sleeping or out.

"Did you love her?" Adam regretted the question as soon as it was out of his mouth, but he couldn't take it back. Knowing that his wife had been having an affair was hard, but knowing that his wife had fallen in love with someone else meant that he had failed as a husband.

"I did. I loved Verona more than I have ever loved anyone. I am sorry for how it happened and the pain it is causing you now, but all I ever wanted was to see her happy." Grant's eyes started to glaze over as he fought back the tears.

"So this leaves one last question. If you loved Verona, and I loved Verona too, and neither of us killed her, who did? Who would have wanted her dead?" The tears fell freely from Adam's face as he wept now, and he made no effort to wipe them away.

"I have no idea." As grant spoke, his receptionist's voice came over the intercom.

"Your next appointment is here."

"Well, I'm sorry I don't have more time, but here's my number. Let's meet up for a drink after office hours, and we can talk more. I'm sorry for what you're going through." Grant led him to the door.

"Talking to you helped." Adam walked out and stopped short when he saw Grant's next patient.

"Stacy?" Adam sounded shocked. "I haven't seen you in years; where have you been?"

Stacy just pushed past him and walked into the office. Adam stood there, watching as Grant closed the door. *I wonder what that was about,* Adam thought.

# CHAPTER SIX

Charlotte and Kristofer had been watching, listening, and waiting for clues for the past week, and when it seemed like they had the same amount of information as the police and nothing more to go on, Charlotte grew impatient. She hadn't yet made herself known to anyone but Grant, and she didn't yet know who would be the most informative. Currently, they were parked outside Adam's house, just observing. They had been watching him for a few days, and the most exciting thing that happened was Adam's visit to Grant's office. Charlotte wanted to ask Grant how the conversation with Adam Sheffield went but was too frustrated to return empty-handed.

The evening sun dipped behind the row of cookie-cutter houses and cast shadows on the street. The lamps lining the sidewalk switched on. It was growing colder as the Midwestern summer came to an end and gave way to autumn. The leaves littered the streets, and occasionally, a gust of wind would kick them up and swirl them in a cyclone that would travel a few feet before dropping back to the ground.

A black car drove slowly down the street, seemingly pausing in front of Adam's house slightly before moving on. Maybe they're looking for an address. Charlotte thought to herself. That thought was pushed from her mind when the car circled the block and drove by again. This time, Charlotte's trained eyes took a mental note of the vehicle's make, model, and license plate. As if they knew that someone had spotted them, the car took off quickly down the street and didn't return.

"Well, it looks like we blew our cover here; what do you say we hit up a 24-hour diner and get some coffee?" Charlotte suggested as she pulled away from the curb.

Charlotte and Kristofer sat in a small booth in the back of the diner, taking in the smell of fry grease and bacon. The restaurant was eerily empty and quiet except for the occasional sound of a banging pot from the kitchen. Their waitress took their orders and disappeared into the back. A whole pot of coffee sat on the table, and Charlotte quickly poured herself a cup, pausing to breathe in the aroma of the fresh brew before preparing it the way she liked. She opened four of the french vanilla creamer cups and added them to her coffee. After taking a sip, she took out her notes and began revisiting what they knew so far.

"So we know that Verona and Adam were high school sweethearts, we know that they married young, began their careers, and later began to drift apart. Verona became involved with her boss and Adam with Milan. We need to find out how long that's been going on. In cases like this, it's usually the jealous husband, and although I can't rule him out, I don't think Adam is our guy." Charlotte rambled. Kristofer loved the way Charlotte had a way of figuring things out, a process that involved going over every detail until the inevitable 'click'. The ah-ha moment.

"I know the librarian at the high school. When we leave here, I want to take a look through their high school yearbooks. We can find out who their friends or even enemies were and go from there."

Kristofer, ever the strong, silent type, nodded and sipped his coffee thoughtfully. Kristofer's dark hair, which he swept off to one side, hung loosely over his left eye, and he had to keep pushing it back out of his face. Charlotte finished her coffee in two large gulps and poured another cup. When they had drunk their fill and were satisfied with the plan, Charlotte hailed the waitress for the tab. Charlotte handed her a ten-dollar bill.

"Keep the change." She called back over her shoulder as they walked out the door. She called the librarian on the way and requested the yearbooks from every year that Adam and Verona attended, five yearbooks in total since Adam was a year older.

They reached the library at Ross Lake High just as the doors opened to allow staff inside. After obtaining visitor passes from the office, Charlotte and Kristofer headed to the library. The books were waiting for them on the counter. Kristofer grabbed them, and Charlotte located an empty table in one of the study rooms where they could look them over without interaction from students that might walk into the library.

Adam and Verona were quite popular. In Adam's senior year, there were many photos of him and Verona together. In one of the images, Adam had his arm around Verona, and she smiled up at him lovingly. She had painted her face in their school colors, and Adam was wearing his football uniform. Nothing stood out about Adam or Verona, but the girl in the background, glaring at them, the look on the girl's face made Charlotte feel uneasy. This girl was not the photo's subject, so there was no reason to list her name beneath it, but Charlotte used her phone to snap a photograph of the page before she slid the book over to Kristofer. She pointed out the girl.

"Might be nothing, could be something. Keep an eye out for her."

Charlotte moved on to Adam's junior year. Adam was a wide receiver for the Ross Lake football team, and he participated in several other clubs.

Adam and Verona were both in the community service project. They posed for a photo at the community Thanksgiving dinner they both spent working, serving community members who had nowhere else to spend the holiday.

Kristofer suddenly lit up over the book he was looking at, Verona's freshman year, which was Adam's sophomore year. He slid the book over to Charlotte.

"Check this out." He pointed out a photo from a football game that showed Verona on the bleachers at a football game and snuggled up to a handsome young man that was not Adam. Charlotte read the names under the photo.

"James Alden. I wonder if the police have talked to him yet?" Charlotte's eyes lit up at the thought of being a step ahead of the local police. She wrote James's name down in her notebook and continued to look through the book from that year. She looked through the collage pages carefully, and suddenly she gasped at the picture on the page. There, standing arm in arm with Adam was the scowling girl from the earlier photo. Immediately Charlotte looked below the image for her name. Stacy Morris. Charlotte wrote that name down and took a picture of that page as well.

"Want to go turn these in for me? It's time to call Paul." Charlotte handed the books to Kristofer. "I will meet you out front." She said as he opened the door to the study room. She was already dialing her phone.

Ten minutes later, Charlotte reached the car with an address pulled up on her phone.

"This Paul guy comes through. Ever going to let me know who he is?" Kristofer looked at his sister with a smug smile suggesting maybe there was more to the story with Paul.

"You know I can't give up the identity of my C.I.," She told him, returning his smile.

They drove to the middle of nowhere, following the directions on Charlotte's phone. After a thirty-minute drive, they pulled onto a dirt driveway leading up to a dilapidated double-wide. A broken-down pickup truck that might have once been red, but was now equal parts rust-brown and primer gray, sat beside the trailer, which looked to be in the same state. The porch was leaning, and all that was keeping the cool fall air and animals out of the house was cardboard, duct tape, and garbage bags.

"This is James Alden's last known address; the information is a couple of years old, so who knows if he still lives here, but worth a shot, right?" Charlotte got out of the car and walked up to the porch, stepping carefully to avoid prominent weak spots and holes in the rotted wood planks. She opened the screen door, which was only attached by the top hinge, and knocked on the inside door. She was about to tap again when heavy footsteps shook the trailer and headed toward the door.

The man who opened it might have been the right age but looked older. His hair had receded so much that only a horseshoe remained around the sides and back of his head; he had a scruffy face and a beer belly that made him look at least a hundred pounds overweight.

"Who er you and whadda ya want?" He asked with a strong Appalachian drawl.

"Are you James Alden?" Charlotte asked.

"I might be, might not be either; that depends on who you are and what ya want."

He made no effort to step out of the doorway and made no effort to allow them inside.

"My name is Georgia Cross; this is Peter. We are investigating the murder of a local woman that Peter knew, and we were hoping he could help us figure out who her other friends were, or more importantly, her enemies." Charlotte said, only lying about their names.

"Well then, I'm afraid I can't help you after all. James doesn't live here. He only had his mail sent here while he was working out of town. Last I heard he was working at the train yard on Wilford Street." With that, he stepped back and closed the door.

Walking back to the car, Kristofer started to laugh.

"What's so funny?"

"Georgia Cross." He laughed again. "Think of your old piano instructor often, do you?"

"It was the first name that came to mind that didn't sound made up. I wasn't going to give him our real names." Charlotte backhanded her brother's chest playfully before he rounded the car to get in. Charlotte pulled up directions to the train yard.

The train yard was across town even after a thirty-minute drive to get back from the middle of nowhere. Charlotte stopped at a gas station to fuel up and grab some drinks. The air was getting chilly outside, so Charlotte made herself a caramel mocha at the touch-screen coffee station. She wandered around the store for a few minutes looking at random merchandise while Kristofer picked out the things he wanted. They approached the counter together, but a sudden urge hit Charlotte.

"Could you take this stuff to the car for me? I have to use the bathroom." She signed "Thank you." to her brother as she hurried off to the ladies

room. Charlotte was humming to herself and trying to think about what she would say to James when she met him. Charlotte's thoughts preoccupied her so much that she didn't hear the footsteps behind her until it was too late. A loud clunk rang through the bathroom, and Charlotte crumpled to the floor.

# CHAPTER SEVEN

Officer Dunn and Officer Jensen had gone over the case together in detail, trying to narrow their focus to one person of interest, but burying the body had bought the killer time. The case notes covered the desk, and Dunn and Jensen kept reading over them again, sure that they were missing something. The weather had washed away much of the evidence there might have been, and Adam Sheffield's home had turned up only clues about the state of their marriage; it had given them little else to go on. Adam seemed honest and in constant despair over his wife's death, and Milan, although cold and unemotional, also appeared too prim and proper to have carried out the act. She had been cooperative enough not to arouse suspicion.

"I tracked down Stacy Morris, that mutual friend that Milan Warren mentioned. I was going to head out and see if we could make contact today. I tried calling, but no answer." Dunn told his partner.

"Do you think Verona was spending time with her, or do you think girl's night was spent with the doctor?" Jensen raised her eyebrows at Dunn.

"Well, it's obvious what you think." He retorted with a smile. "Still, we should follow up on every lead." Dunn grabbed the keys and headed for the door with Jensen right behind, but before they reached the door, the dispatcher called them back.

"A woman was just assaulted in the bathroom of the gas station on route 50."

"We'll check it out." He replied and nodded to Jensen, confirming the change of plans.

When they got to the scene, there were people gathered outside. The gas station attendant had locked the door, so they had to knock. One of the employees looked to see who wanted to enter, and when he saw that it was the police, he opened the door for them and then locked it back as soon as they entered. The victim was sitting up, holding a bag of ice, wrapped in a towel, to the back of her head. Her injury had caused a big red stain on the towel, and Dunn hoped that it was not as bad as it appeared.

When the ambulance arrived, Dunn and Jensen excused themselves to look for evidence. Jensen went to the bathroom and Dunn to the manager's office.

The manager logged into the camera system so that Dunn could get a view of the scene and their possible suspect.

"You select the date here." He said, pointing the cursor at the drop-down menu at the top of the screen. "This brings up the whole day from midnight to right now. Then, just like you're playing a video, you can fast forward, rewind, or pause." The manager stepped aside to let Dunn have control.

"Thanks... Greg." He had to look at the man's name tag because they skipped introductions.

Greg nodded and left the office so Dunn could look through the feed.


Jensen looked at the drops of blood on the bathroom floor and then looked in every stall. Other than the blood, nothing immediately stood out, so Jensen returned to the victim.

"How are you doing?" Jensen asked as the EMT stepped away from Charlotte.

"I suppose I have been better." Charlotte managed a smile.

"I'm officer Jensen." She held out her hand to Charlotte.

"Charlotte Bradley." She replied, taking Jensen's hand.

"Can you tell me what happened, Charlotte?"

"When I finished using the restroom, someone hit me in the head from behind as I walked out of the stall."

"Did you happen to see anything? A weapon, or maybe a reflection in the mirror." Suggested Jensen.

"No, I hadn't reached the mirror yet, and it all happened so fast."

"Did your attacker take anything from you?"

"No, they left all of my belongings... wait." Charlotte reached for her cell phone and opened her image gallery; her heart sank. The yearbook photos were gone. She went to the trash icon and found that whoever went to the trouble of deleting them didn't empty the trash. She selected the photos and restored them to the gallery.

"This has something to do with Verona Warren-Sheffield," Charlotte said.

"What do you mean?" Jensen's surprise was evident at the mention of Verona's name.

"I'm a private investigator. Someone hired me to find out who killed Verona. I was following up on a lead." Charlotte showed the picture of Verona with James Alden. "I was on my way to talk to this guy, James Alden, when the attacker hit me."

Dunn walked out of the office. "The suspect obscured their face. It appears to be a woman, I'm guessing, from her size and frame. She came in wearing a hooded sweatshirt and sunglasses. I printed some photos, but without being able to see her face, I'm not sure they will do much good. We will post them on our Social page to see if the public can identify them."

Jensen repeated Charlotte's story to Dunn. Charlotte showed him the photo of James Alden.

"Well, how about we get you back in tip-top shape, and then we will go see James together," Dunn suggested. "The more minds we have on this, the better."

While Charlotte rested, Kristofer exchanged their rental car. He couldn't risk someone following them; it was apparent that whoever attacked Charlotte knew what kind of car they were driving. Kristofer picked up lunch for the two of them before returning to the hotel where they had been staying. When he got into the room, he found Charlotte sleeping comfortably in one of the double beds. He turned on the TV but turned the volume down, so he didn't disturb Charlotte's sleep.

Charlotte slept all that day and into the night. When she woke up, she was hungry, and her throat was as dry as the desert sand. Charlotte reached for the water bottle on the bedside table and drank the whole thing without stopping.

"How long was I asleep?" She looked over at Kristofer, who was sitting on his bed with Charlotte's notes spread out in front of him.

"It's been about 12 hours now." He told her. "Welcome back." He said with a smile. Charlotte's eyes wandered around the room, and she squinted her eyes as they adjusted to the light of the room. Their room was a cookie-cutter hotel room, similar to every other cheap accommodation, with floral bedspreads, a reddish-orange accent wall, and that ugly geometrical carpet that reminded Charlotte of 'The Shining.'

"My head is killing me. Would you grab the pain reliever from my bag?" Charlotte pointed to the bag beside the dresser that she had still not unpacked. Kristofer handed her the pills and then grabbed her water bottle to fill it up again.

"You're too good to me, little brother; what would I do without you?" She forced a smile through the pain.

"Probably get yourself into even more trouble than you do already." He laughed and shook his head at Charlotte.

"So what do we do next?" Charlotte asked, nodding toward the note-covered bed.

"Officer Dunn said he would check in tomorrow, and if you're feeling up to it, he would like to go talk to James Alden with us." Kristofer began shuffling the papers together to put them back into the manila folder Charlotte had them in.

Charlotte couldn't stop thinking about her attacker. She wondered if she had passed them in the store as she shopped or why that person would go through all the trouble to delete a couple of yearbook photos from her phone. Nothing about the pictures was incriminating, which made Charlotte feel like maybe they had stumbled a little too close.

Charlotte took out her phone and the card that Dunn had given her with his number on it. She looked at the time; it was only seven-thirty. A few moments later, Charlotte had Dunn on the phone explaining her feeling and coordinating their next plan of action. It was a rare occasion that local police were accepting of her snooping around open cases, but it seemed like this case was on the verge of going cold until now.

Dunn said he would assign a detail to James and Stacy. He made Charlotte promise to, at the very least, take the night off. She agreed, but as soon as they hung up, she grabbed her laptop and began making a flier with her burner phone number listed on it. Charlotte offered housekeeping services at affordable prices, then created a Social page for her phony business. She posted deliberately on Milan Warren's page and Madeline's art page.

It didn't even take a full twenty-four hours; Madeleine called her the very next morning and asked if she would be willing to clean their house.

Charlotte arrived with newly purchased cleaning supplies around nine in the morning. Madeline showed her inside and gave her a quick tour.

"I will be in my studio if you need anything," Madeline said. She turned, and her heels echoed down the hall. The house looked more like a museum with its black and white contemporary decor, paintings, and sculptures in every room.

Charlotte dusted, disinfected, vacuumed, and mopped each room. When she got to Henry's office she pushed the door so that it was left open only a crack. She went straight to his computer and pressed the space bar. Immediately, the input bar came up for the password. Charlotte tried a few with no luck. She gave up on the computer and moved to the bookshelf that sat along the western wall. Charlotte pulled out the books one by one, flipping through the pages like a Vegas dealer shuffling cards. Halfway through the shelf, she opened a large book, and photos fell out of it, scattering to the floor in a pile. They were photos of a girl's body. Her face was not visible in any of the images, but in some of them, she was naked and tied up, and in some, she was wearing a leather corset, garters, and a black lace bra that left very little to the imagination. *This isn't Madeline.* Charlotte thought. When Charlotte picked up the last photo, she gasped. In this one, Henry was tied to his office chair with black rope, and he had a pair of black lacy panties stuffed into his mouth. She used her phone to snap pictures of the evidence she found and then quickly put it all back where she had found it. Charlotte finished cleaning, her heart pounding out of her chest the whole time. She couldn't get out of there fast enough; as soon as Madeline had paid her and given her a very generous tip.

Charlotte headed back to the hotel and only breathed a sigh of relief when she saw Kristofer waiting for her.

"You'll never believe what I found." She said.

# CHAPTER EIGHT

Friday night, Milan sat at her parents' dining room table scrolling through her phone. Her parents had been bugging her even more than usual lately to come over for family dinner. Milan was not impressed, which was not unusual. There were a million other things she would rather be doing with her Friday night but Milan's mother, Madeline, had made chicken and penne pasta with a home-made vodka sauce, or more likely, she had their personal chef, Helen cook it because it was Milan's favorite. Milan had felt too guilty to say no.

"Please, put your phone down, honey. We invited you for dinner to spend time with you." Madeline said.

"Sorry, Mom," Milan said as she slid her phone into her pocket. She picked at her food, took small bites here and there, and seemed to be avoiding eye contact. It was quiet, Henry, Milan's dad was eating without making conversation and the look on his face told Milan he had no plans to change that.

"What's wrong?" Madeline asked.

"Nothing," Milan responded.

"Come on, something is bothering you, I can tell, you have barely said two words to us in the last hour." Her mother pressed the issue. Milan became aggravated as her mother continued. The more she denied anything being wrong, the more her mother pressed on.

"You've barely said two words to me in the last *year* until now! If Verona hadn't gotten herself murdered, you probably still wouldn't have. Now that I'm the only kid you have left, suddenly you want to make an effort!" Milan was screaming at this point and shoved herself away from the table and rushed from the dining room. Madeline and Henry both looked after her in complete shock. Milan hadn't meant to get emotional tonight but being at that table, alone with her parents, reality hit her like a ton of bricks.

Milan was hyperventilating when she dialed the phone. She didn't know who else to call, so she called Adam. She shouldn't have, she knew that. He had asked for space, but she really needed him right now. It went straight to voicemail. *Come on, Adam!* Milan thought as she hung up and dialed again. Once more, it went directly to voicemail.

Madeline came into the room and tried to put her arm around Milan, but her daughter shrugged away her comfort.

"I'm sorry that I haven't been around much. I know I get into my own world sometimes with my art, but I always love you, and I'm always here for you." Madeline's eyes met Milan's pleading with her.

"Where were you when Roman died?" Milan accused.

"Your father and I were in Paris at a gallery opening. We flew home as soon as we heard."

"You missed the funeral!" Milan screamed. "Have you ever thought about, or wondered who killed Verona? It doesn't seem like you even care." Milan continued screaming and Madeline stood there with tears streaming down her face.

Milan stopped as her father walked into the room and glared at her.

"Get out." He said, pointing toward the door. "Maybe the reason your mother doesn't try to contact you more is that you treat her like this. Go. We have no children left." His voice was unwavering and his words stung. Milan took one final look back at her parents before storming off, slamming the door behind her.

Milan tried to call Adam again. Voicemail. She screamed and banged her fist against the steering wheel, blaring the horn as she did. She felt so angry and rejected by not only her own parents but now Adam too. Her whole life everyone preferred Verona. Her parents liked Verona best, Adam had fallen in love with her, and all of their teachers in school always praised her. When Roman was alive though, he was Milan's biggest fan. Roman had been her best friend. Milan sat in her car with tears free flowing as she held close the memories of her brother.

Roman and Milan were only nine months apart but many people thought they were twins from the time they were six and seven until Roman died. The two of them were always together and really didn't care much for socializing with other people.

Roman liked his hair long. It was dark brown and made his green eyes stand out. He had a nineties grunge style- black jeans with holes in the knees, black t-shirts, and a flannel shirt that was usually tied around his waist. He had been popular with the girls in school but he had never taken an interest in anyone in particular. He preferred to spend all of his time with Milan. They had thought he was delayed because he never spoke to anyone but Milan until first grade. Due to this, they had started his schooling a year late and he and Milan had been in the same grade, which is likely the reason everyone thought they were twins.

The Warrens paid for private schooling for their children in elementary school, which gave them more control over their education. Roman had had a speech therapist for his first year of school attend class with him to encourage him to use his words. Still, he would only talk to Milan.

When Roman did finally begin talking to others, he talked with a slight lisp and a stutter. His speech therapist saw him twice a week once he was verbal, and eventually, the lisp went away but sometimes, when he was very angry, the stutter would come back.

As they got older, Roman taught Milan brotherly things, like how to stand up for herself in a fight and how to shoot a bow. He also took her fishing and hunting regularly in the woods behind their house. They mostly killed squirrels and rabbits, and always ate what they took.

Verona had dance, and music lessons so she was very rarely home to explore with them. Roman and Milan found that they were left with the caretaker often while their mother, or Helen when their mother was away for work, took Verona all over town for her various extracurricular activities. They didn't mind, they preferred it this way for several years. They didn't start spending time away from each other until middle school.

Milan made friends and became interested in boys. Roman made friends and also became interested in boys.

When Roman got his license, he was hardly ever home. He had saved up his allowance, Christmas, and birthday money to buy a car and it was a nice one too. He bought a jet-black sports car. It was a convertible and the very first time Roman took Milan for a ride in it, they drove with the top down on the freeway. Milan didn't foresee the danger and had applauded her brother's choice in transportation. She kept thinking about how cool they would look driving it to school, and how everyone in school was going to want to ride with them.

The night Roman died, Milan had begged him to take her to a party on the other side of town. Their parents were in France and the caretaker always left after dinner. Roman agreed because he could never deny his favorite sister anything. Verona was spending the night with Adam so Roman thought it might be fun to go to the party for a little while.

The party was just like every other teenage party, beer and booze flowing, kids dancing, some making out in the corners, who knows what was going on in the bedrooms upstairs, and of course, there was a pool. Roman and Milan went their separate ways, got drinks, and began mingling. Several hours went by before Roman stumbled up to Milan, drunk, and told her it was time to go home. Milan had been making out with Chris Jacobs at the time and protested. Roman tried to insist but Chris spoke up and offered to drive Milan home.

"Fine," Roman said, but it wasn't fine. Milan knew he was angry but he left without her just the same. She went back to making out with Chris and put Roman out of her mind for the night. When Chris dropped her off, Milan's eyes darted right to the driveway. *Roman Still isn't home.* She began to worry that he might get himself into trouble because of his temper, she worried even more that he might be mad at her.

Milan distressed all that night, pacing the floor, checking the phone, and waiting for Roman to come home. When there was finally a knock on the door, a boulder dropped in Milan's stomach. She had a feeling that something was wrong. Her feeling was confirmed when she opened the door to two officers who immediately removed their hats and held them with their arms crossed in the front.

"May I speak with Madeline or Henry Warren please?" They asked.

"They're in France." Milan looked expectantly.

"Are you Roman Warren's sister?"

Milan nodded because the words caught in her throat and she couldn't speak. The tears had already begun welling up in her eyes at the sound of his name coming from the officers.

"There's been an accident. A bad one. His car exploded. The fire burned the body. The license plate was the only way we could identify him until we get his remains ran for DNA."

Milan screamed and fell to her knees sobbing. She felt that the gods if there were any at all, must have hated her. To take her favorite person in the world from her, and then on top of it, she alone, had to hear the news. The officers spoke some more, but she didn't hear a word of it. When they finished speaking, they showed themselves out.

Milan Called Verona home from Adam's and told her the news. They finally got word to their parents in France and quick arrangements were made for a funeral service, even though Roman's Body was gone. The Warrens promised they would be back in time, but their flight caught turbulence in a storm and suffered some lightning damage. They had to land and change planes in Denver, which caused them to miss the funeral. Milan and Verona were left to deal with that pain alone.

Now, this pain was different. This pain was caused by knowing that the only person who ever loved her was long dead, and her sister, who tolerate her had been murdered. Her father's words came back to haunt her. "We have no children left."

She saw red, She punched her right foot down on the gas pedal in her car, and her head plastered to the headrest as the car jolted forward. She kept pressing the pedal to the floor and the speedometer kept climbing, sixty, seventy, eighty... Milan couldn't even see where she was going she could only feel. All the hate she held in her heart was pouring out of her foot and onto the gas pedal. Still, the car went faster, ninety, one hundred, one-ten...

Then she was flying. The car flew right off the side of the bluff overlooking Ross Lake. Her stomach jumped into her throat as the car became weightless in the air and paused in the sky before it started pointing down. Roman flashed before her eyes and nothing else mattered. She closed her eyes and embraced the end as her car fell down, farther and farther, until the icy waters of Ross Lake claimed it.

As her car slowly sank, she found herself watching the crash from the shore as bubbles rose from the depths and popped on the surface of the water. She watched until the bubbles stopped and the lake was still and calm as if nothing had happened. When the bubbles were gone, the world disappeared. Only darkness remained.

# CHAPTER NINE

Adam woke up next to an empty bottle of whiskey. He felt around the bed for his phone and tried to check the time, but the battery was dead. Adam fumbled around, following the cord to could plug it into his phone. As soon as the green battery charging screen popped up reading zero percent, he let his head fall back down to the pillow with a groan.

It took all the energy he could muster to pull himself out of bed and to the shower. Adam stood in the heavy stream with his back to the spray, letting the water massage his muscles and ease the pounding in his head. Once he finished, he wrapped a towel around his lower half and walked to the kitchen to put on a pot of coffee. From his bedroom, he heard his phone start, and then the notifications started.

He looked at his phone and noticed two missed calls from Milan. He tried to call her back, but the only answer he got said, *"The person you are trying to reach has a mailbox that has not been set up." It figures.* Adam thought. If she didn't answer her phone, it was because she didn't want to talk to you. He tried again. *She's probably trying to pay me back for last night.* Adam thought that he put his phone back down so it could charge.

Adam did his usual weekend morning routine, and when he finished, he tried to call Milan again only to be greeted by the automated voice once more. *Okay, enough of this. You've made your point, Milan.* Adam decided he would have to drive over to her house. As much as he hoped to avoid spending time with her until the police finished investigating, he found that his heart secretly ached for Milan. Although their affair had started months before Verona's death, having someone to share the burden with made him feel safe.

When Adam reached Milan's house, he found her not at home. She sometimes worked weekends when there was a deadline she had to meet for the magazine, so Adam drove to her office. The parking spot reserved for the CEO was empty. Adam parked, checked his reflection in the rearview mirror, and then popped a breath mint to cover the smell of any stale alcohol that his toothpaste hadn't eliminated. The lobby was buzzing with activity, and phones were ringing at almost every desk. Adam approached the receptionist.

"Has Milan been in today?"

The young woman behind the desk wore a black and white pantsuit and minimal makeup. Her features made her look young, possibly eighteen, and on her first internship. She lifted her face from her computer screen to look Adam over as he placed his hand on the counter in front of her.

"I'm sorry, Sir, she has not come in yet today." She tried to keep her face from giving anything away, but Adam saw the worry in her expression.

"Is something wrong? She is my sister-in-law." He hated the way that sounded as soon as it left his mouth. He knew they weren't related but just saying that out loud made his stomach turn a little.

The woman looked at Adam again. "I haven't been able to reach her this morning."

"Would you try again, please?" *Maybe she would answer for the magazine. Perhaps it was just him she was avoiding.*

The receptionist picked up the phone and dialed it but hung up a moment later, which told Adam that she had received the same message that he had earlier. *Her phone is never off.* Adam began to worry. A million thoughts raced through his mind, but the first thought was about Madeline and Henry. He ran back to his car and drove a little too quickly to The Warren's home.

Adam frantically knocked on their front door. He paced on the porch as he waited for the sound of approaching footsteps. When Madeline answered the door, she immediately rushed out to wrap an arm around Adam's shoulder.

"What's wrong, Adam?" She asked, leading him inside.

"Have you heard from Milan today?" Adam asked,

"No, I'm sorry. Milan left here last night after an argument with her father. He was angry and said some things, Milan said things, and then she left. I was hoping to give her some time and smooth things over this week." She studied Adam's face. "What... You don't think something has happened, do you?" She covered her mouth with both hands and started shaking her head.

"Before you can file a missing person's report, they will require her to be gone for seventy-two hours. If you don't hear from her by then, please call the police. I will keep looking for her in the meantime." Adam knew how it would look if he went to the police with this. He knew they were still going to suspect him no matter who reported it, but he thought it would look better coming from her parents. Adam stood to leave but turned back to Madeline. "If you hear from her, please call and let me know. I will be sure to do the same."

Adam drove around town, checking all of the places he knew Milan liked, but he didn't see her car anywhere. The sky was gray and dark, even though it was only midday. The weather had gotten cold a lot sooner than it had last year, and the weatherman had predicted an early winter with the first snowfall within the next couple of days. Adam thought about how they had found Verona's body. *If the ground freezes and everything gets covered in snow, it would be next spring before they find a body now.* Adam detested these thoughts, but he couldn't push them away because what if whoever killed Verona did the same thing to Milan? Adam started to cry and had to pull over because he couldn't see through the tears.

Adam wiped his eyes and gave himself a pep talk. *Get your shit together, come on, where would she go?* He got back on the road. *It's getting cold; when it's cold, Milan likes to go where it's warm.*

Adam drove until he reached the airport. He searched through the parking garage and the parking lot with no luck finding Milan's car. Adam searched for hours, and it was getting dark and hard to see the details of vehicles from a distance. He admitted that it would be impossible to find her in the dark and decided that he should head home and get some sleep. This way, he could get up early tomorrow morning to continue the search.

On his way home, Adam drove past Milan's again. Her house was dark, and the driveway empty. He felt just how the house looked; abandoned. When he got home, Adam went right to bed, but sleep eluded him. His mind became flooded with thoughts of Milan and Verona. Adam thought about how lucky he had been to love both of them and how unlucky he had been to lose them. Then, he thought about how the primary thing they had in common was him. Maybe he was a curse on their family.

A sound brought Adam out of his self-loathing. It sounded like someone walking down the hall to his bedroom. Adam opened his bedside drawer and pulled out his 9mm. He loaded it and got out of bed. The footsteps in the hallway were closer now, and Adam slowly crept to the door frame. He tried to peek around the corner but saw only darkness. Adam slid out the doorway and into the hall. When he exhaled, his breath came out as a white cloud and hung in the air. Holding the pistol with one hand and fumbling for the light with the other, Adam managed to flip the switch to illuminate an empty hallway.

"Who are you?" Adam called out. The curtains blew wildly from the front window in the living room, casting dancing shadows throughout the space. Adam let out a sigh of relief. *I'm so tired. That must be why I'm hearing things.* He moved to close the window, and just as he stepped in front of it, a gust of wind pushed him backward, and Adam's bedroom door slammed shut, causing him to jump and whirl around.

Adam closed the window as quickly as he could and then went back to his bedroom. Adam grabbed his sleep aid from the drawer and took two. Just as he reached for the light switch, the light above him began to flicker, and the bedroom door slammed closed again, causing him to gasp as he whirled around to face it. Adam's heart pounded in his chest as he reached for the knob. The whole door started to rattle. Adam stumbled as he backed away from it. *This isn't real; I'm dreaming.* Adam thought as he slid to the floor in the corner of the room. He put his head on his knees and squeezed his eyes shut tight.

Soon silence filled the room, and even the buzz from the flickering light was gone. Adam opened his eyes to total darkness. Adam stood and felt his way across the room to the light switch.

It was in the on position. He flipped it down and flipped it back on; the light did not come on. Adam felt his way around the edge of the bed and to the closet. Adam grabbed the flashlight he kept on the shelf. He shined it on the door, which remained motionless.

The house was quiet. Adam jerked the door open and shined the light down the hall. He turned on every lamp and switch from the hallway to the kitchen. Adam grabbed an extra light bulb from under the sink and made his way back to his room. Nothing seemed out of place, and the more time went by, the more he tried to convince himself that it didn't happen.

Adam took the cover off the light and replaced the bulb. As soon as the room illuminated, Adam was face to face with a screaming Verona; only she was covered in dirt and half decomposed. She reached out a dirty hand to Adam, but he was frozen with fear as his dead wife stood before him. She moved forward and pushed her fingers into his forehead. He fell backward, and everything went black as he crumpled to the floor.

# CHAPTER TEN

James Alden looked precisely the same now as he had in his yearbook photo. Charlotte noticed his ageless features, full hair, and squared jawline with just enough of a five o'clock shadow to distinguish him from his teenage portrait. Charlotte, Kristofer, Dunn, and Jensen had found James at work. Once Dunn and Jensen presented their badges, they had no trouble getting someone to point out James to them.

"James Alden?" Dunn's inflection indicated this was a question, but it was rhetorical. He knew this to be James.

"Yes, Sir. How can I help you?" He stopped what he was doing to look at them.

"Is there a private place we can talk? We just wanted to ask you some questions about Verona Warren-Sheffield." Jensen looked at James sympathetically. James nodded and led them to the office. He grabbed a couple of extra folding chairs from the closet and made sure everyone had a place to sit before taking a seat behind the desk.

"I heard what happened to Verona. It's a shame." James said. "How can I possibly help?"

"Did you know of anyone who might have wanted to hurt Verona?" Jensen asked. Charlotte was taking notes in her notebook as they spoke.

"In high school, back when I knew her, I would say no. Everyone loved her. She was popular, fun, and nice, which is a rare quality in that crowd." James told them.

"Can you tell us about this photo?" Jensen passed the photograph of James and Verona across the desk. James smiled. "Sure. This photo is from our first date. I had asked her to come to the game with me, and I couldn't believe she had said yes. Her sister set us up. I used to have the biggest crush on Verona's sister, Milan, but she didn't feel the same. She set me up with Verona instead."

"How long did you guys date?" Dunn asked,

"Maybe a year."

"Were you angry when she broke up with you?"

"Actually, I broke up with her. That's my biggest regret from high school." A look of embarrassment crossed James' face as he admitted it.

"Can you tell us what happened? Why did you break up with her?" Jensen looked genuinely interested in the story.

"I was young and dumb. I joined the football team, and there were a *lot* of pretty cheerleaders. I wanted to play the field a little bit before getting tied down. I felt that things were maybe getting too serious, and so I told her we should see other people."

"How did she take it?"

"Honestly, I don't know. If Verona was upset at all, she never let me see it; Adam Sheffield was right there to lend his shoulder to cry on, though, and they ended up getting married so, I guess it all worked out. Well, until now, that is." James's expression saddened.

"What about this picture?" Jensen slid him the picture of Adam and Stacy Morris.

"Stacy was obsessed with Adam. I heard that Adam even cheated on her, and she still wanted him. Stacy dropped off the face of the planet senior year, and no one knew where she went, although there was a rumor that she tried to kill herself and her parents had her committed. Stacy turned up a few years after that, partying in all the bars. The last time I saw her was on New Year's Eve. I had a party at my place to celebrate the new year and a new beginning, you know since I had just bought a new house."

Charlotte wrote all of this down. Dunn and Jensen exchanged a glance at each other.

"Thank you so much for your time, James. If you think of anything else, give us a call." Jensen handed him a card, and his fingers brushed hers as he took it. He smiled as her fingers lingered in his for a moment before she pulled away and turned toward the door so he wouldn't see the blush that had risen to her cheeks. Dunn, however, shot her a knowing glance.

When they reached the parking lot, Dunn stopped the others before they could get into their vehicles. "Is anyone else feeling like maybe this Stacy Morris is a good lead?" Dunn's voice was almost a whisper, and everyone had to lean in close to hear him.

"Do you know where to find her?" Jensen asked.

"No, but remember, Milan said that Stacy was a mutual friend and that you could learn a lot from someone's Social page." He pulled out his phone and looked up Stacy's profile. As he scrolled through her page, he noticed that she had not updated in five years and only ever shared memes when she did. She never posted a self-written status or even a picture of herself. When he pointed this out, Jensen offered a thought on the matter.

"Usually, that means that the poster doesn't want anyone to know what they look like; maybe this is a sign. Could be drugs, or maybe Stacy gained a bunch of weight and didn't want everyone from high school to know." Jensen said.

"Maybe Stacy turned to a life of crime and needs to keep her identity a secret because of that," Charlotte added. "I will do some digging and see what I find."

"When we get back to the station, I will run her info through the system and see if I get a hit," Dunn said.

They left the train yard and set out on their separate tasks. Dunn and Jensen went back to the station and began searching their database for information.

The system turned up very little on Stacy Morris, no DMV record, no arrests, and vital statistics didn't even have a birth certificate on file. That didn't mean much, though; she might have been born somewhere else, at least Jensen seemed to think so. Jensen always had a positive attitude. She still saw the good in people and situations, despite the nature of her job. Sometimes Dunn wondered what on earth made her want to become a police officer, especially in a little town like Ross Lake where the same officer who issued parking tickets could be solving a murder the next day.

Jensen had been twenty-one when she entered the police academy, and in thirteen weeks, her training was complete, and they had assigned Dunn to be her partner. She loved working with officer Dunn, or Harry, as she sometimes called him when they were off the clock. Dunn was a little taller than she was, a lot rounder, and had a lot more gray hair. He was in his late fifties now, so that wasn't unusual. Jensen wanted to become a police officer ever since she could remember. She had wanted to help people, solve crimes, and see justice done. Someday, she planned on making the rank of detective, but for now, being just an officer was okay with her.

"What do we do now?" Jensen asked Dunn as he searched on the ancient desktop computer that sat on his desk.

"We look up everyone she went to school with to see if anyone knows her whereabouts. We can also request her enrollment records from the school." Dunn replied.

"Get Milan on the phone, see if she knows how to reach Stacy. She did say they were friends after all." Jensen suggested.

Dunn immediately started dialing. After a moment, he hung up and then dialed again. He repeated the action a few times, checking the number between each dial to ensure correctness.

"Strange, it says that she never set up her voicemail," Dunn said, looking at his phone with confusion. Dunn grabbed his coat and keys, then headed for the door. Jensen followed quickly after, extending her stride to match his pace.

Dunn and Jensen pulled up outside Milan's townhouse about ten minutes later. Her car wasn't there, but they knocked on the door anyway. When Milan didn't answer, they continued their inquiries elsewhere. Days passed, and Dunn felt like they were no closer to Stacy than they were before. They were also no closer to solving Verona's murder, and they *still* hadn't made contact with Milan.

Dunn crossed off two more names from Stacy's graduating class. These two he had found in the obituaries. Dunn had spent the morning reaching out to everyone who might have known Stacy from school. He was close to deciding he needed a break when his phone rang. It was Mrs. Warren, calling to report Milan missing.

# CHAPTER ELEVEN

James Alden got home from work that evening, still thinking about his encounter with the police. Notably, Officer Jensen. He pulled the card out of his pocket and thought about calling her. James didn't have any information to offer, and he was worried that he had misread the situation. *Had there been a spark between us, or am I just hoping?* He asked himself. He turned the card over in his hands a few times before putting it back inside his wallet. *Another day, perhaps.*

James walked to the kitchen and heated some leftovers from the refrigerator. The kitchen was silent, except for the beeping as he pressed buttons on the microwave and the hum that followed after he pressed the start button. A few minutes later, James was sitting at the table with a spaghetti plate in front of him. He had only taken one bite when his dinner was interrupted by a knock at his back door. James looked up from his plate, confused because no one ever came to the back door; the backyard had a privacy fence around it. He got up to answer, and as he did, the knocking became more urgent. When he swung the door open, James was shocked to see Stacy push her way into his house.

She looked different than when he saw her last; she had cut and dyed her hair; now it was shoulder-length and blonde. Her clothes were baggy, and the hood on her sweatshirt obscured her face in shadow.

"Stacy, what are you doing here?"

Stacy looked at him and then pushed past him to the living room. She curled up on his couch and drifted off to sleep. James couldn't tell if Stacy was high or drunk, so he just stared at her in disbelief. As she slept, James quietly stepped outside the back door. He took Jensen's card out of his wallet and called her. He told her that Stacy had shown up at his house and was asleep on his couch. Jensen promised to be there soon and asked him to keep her there.

James walked back into the kitchen nervously, half expecting Stacy to be gone, but she still slept on the couch. James paced across the kitchen. The wait seemed to last forever, but finally, he heard a car turn onto his street and stop in front of the house. He watched from the window and opened the door before Jensen or Dunn had a chance to knock and wake his uninvited guest.

When Jensen saw Stacy, she recognized her at once. The look on Dunn's face told her that he did too. Stacy woke and screamed in shock as Dunn flipped her off the couch and started cuffing her.

"You're under arrest for the assault of Charlotte Bradley. You have the right to remain silent; anything you say can and *will* be used against you in a court of law. You have the right to an attorney; if you cannot afford an attorney, one will be appointed to you. Do you understand these rights as I have read them to you?"

Stacy stayed silent but shot James a threatening look as Dunn pulled her to her feet and ushered her to the door. James's hands were shaking, and the color had drained from his face. Jensen reached out and took his hand in hers.

"You did the right thing." She smiled and patted his hand. "Call me if you need anything." Jensen let his hand go, but he held on to her a moment longer, looking into her eyes with a combination of fear and longing. Her cheeks flushed, and she turned quickly so that he wouldn't notice and followed Dunn out the door.

James followed her to the door and watched her until the car was out of sight. *You idiot, you should have said something.* He scolded himself. James made it a personal goal to work up the courage to ask her out by the end of the week. Once they left, James went back to his spaghetti. It was cold now, and he had left it sitting too long. James scraped it into the disposal and decided that he wasn't hungry after all.

James spent the evening laying on the couch, watching television. He couldn't sleep after the day he had. It was after midnight when a knock at his door startled him. He almost fell off the couch as he jumped to his feet. His heart was pounding as he walked to the door, expecting a furious Stacy.

The dread washed away when he opened the door, instead, to Officer Jensen. She wasn't in uniform. Her long brown hair hung to her waist in soft curls, and her eyes glittered under his porch light. James's voice caught at the sight of her, and he had to clear his throat before he could speak.

"Officer Jensen, is everything okay?"

"I'm off duty, please, call me Sara." she stepped closer, looking up at him. James let a low groan escape his lips, and he couldn't resist any longer. He wrapped his arms around her waist and pulled her into a deep and needful kiss as she started tugging at his shirt. Their lips broke apart long enough for her to pull his t-shirt over his head. James pushed the front door closed as he pulled Sara into his living room. Like a magnet, his lips found hers again and then trailed down her neck as he slipped her brown leather jacket off her shoulders and let it drop to the floor. The dress she wore underneath was silky and clung to her. James's hands explored the curves of her body as they moved toward the sofa. James looked at her, admiring her shape and beauty.

"Sara." As he whispered her name, he saw the tingle go through her from the goosebumps that appeared on her arms.

He slid the spaghetti straps of her dress off her shoulders and unhooked her strapless bra. The silky material flowed to her feet and pooled around them, still warm from the heat of her body. James pulled back to take in the sight of her, exhaling sharply at the image of her body bared before him and the tightness in his pants that he could no longer endure. At that exact moment, she seemed to realize that he was still wearing too many articles of clothing, and she began unbuttoning his pants.

Once she had undressed him completely, James pulled Sara toward the couch and then on top of him as he sat down, never moving his eyes from hers. He kissed her deeply, tugging gently at her bottom lip with his teeth. His lips explored her neck, then her chest, and when his mouth found her nipple, he flicked it with his tongue. They made love for hours that night, and at some point, they moved from the sofa to James's bed. They fell asleep satisfied and woke up, still tangled together like vines.

James awoke first, and he stared in disbelief at the beautiful woman asleep in his arms. He held her tightly and kissed her forehead. She stirred in his arms and opened her eyes. Instead of the beautiful moment, James had expected, Sara sat up quickly and startled him.

"What time is it?" She asked as she jumped up and began dressing as quickly as she could.

"It's half-past six," James told her.

"Shit, I'm going to be late. I have to go." She kissed him quickly and rushed from his room. James stayed in his bed and listened as his front door closed and a car started, then the engine roared as Sara drove down the street.

# CHAPTER TWELVE

Adam walked into the Ross Lake police department, although he didn't know why. His mind felt far away, and the world was a hazy vision, blackened around the edges as if he saw it through the eyes of another. He walked up to the receptionist's desk and heard his voice ask for the detective in charge of Verona Sheffield's case. An officer pointed to Dunn's desk. Adam stopped suddenly in his approach and collapsed to the ground with a sickening crack. His body writhed and his back arched. Everyone stopped and observed the scene in shock until Dunn shouted.

"He's having a seizure; quick, someone, call an ambulance!" Dunn dropped beside Adam and rolled him onto his side. Then he moved the chairs away from the desk and grabbed his jacket from the back of his chair. Dunn rolled his coat into a pillow and used it to support Adam's head. Adam's body stopped twitching and was now motionless. Adam was unresponsive.

The ambulance arrived, and the paramedics loaded Adam into the back. The fluorescent lights overhead began to flicker as the ambulance left. Dunn looked up at them, and they stopped. A chill blew through the building as they closed the front doors again, trapping a gust inside. Dunn grabbed his jacket and put it on. He shivered as it warmed his body.

When Jensen arrived, Dunn approached her and filled her in on the events that took place moments before her arrival.

"That's crazy! Is he okay?" Jensen asked.

"I'm not sure. I will call the hospital tomorrow." Dunn said. "Are you ready to interview Stacy? Her lawyer should be here soon."

"Court-appointed?" Jensen asked. Dunn nodded and began leading the way to the elevator.

The basement was a little colder than the upstairs was. Dunn wondered if maybe he was starting to catch a cold. He pulled his jacket tighter and approached the guard at the desk.

"We are here to interview Stacy Morris," Jensen told the officer who was seated in the comfortable-looking chair behind the desk. He looked at them, then pointed to the log for visitors to sign in.

Dunn and Jensen filled out the required fields, and then the man behind the desk buzzed them into the cell block. Two guards went to get Stacy as Dunn and Jensen made their way to the interrogation room. When they brought Stacy into the room, Dunn noticed the bruises on her face.

"What happened to her?" He demanded to the guards.

"She became violent this morning like she was fighting the air, then she started banging her head on the walls. We had to sedate her. She's still medicated, but she is responsive." The guards sat her down and cuffed her to the chair; then, they exited the room. Dunn could see them standing just outside the door, waiting for them to finish.

"You can tell me what happened. I can help you." Dunn motioned to Stacy's face. Stacy looked to the floor and didn't speak. A moment later, the guards escorted Stacy's lawyer into the room.

"I hope you're not trying to talk to my client before I'm present, Mr. Dunn," he said as he found his seat and opened his briefcase on the table in front of him. "I'm Frank Holland, and I will be representing Miss Morris. My first question is, has she had a psychological appointment yet?"

"Not yet. It's scheduled for tomorrow morning." Dunn said.

"Well then, I am afraid this meeting is over for right now until we determine her mentally competent to withstand questioning. I don't know about you, but she hasn't spoken a word to me. That signifies some mental trauma. It is my professional recommendation that we have these issues assessed and documented before we proceed further. Would you agree?"

Dunn started to protest, but he knew it would be a lost cause. The expression on his face showed his anger as he stood and nodded to Mr. Holland and walked abruptly from the room.

Jensen followed behind, letting the guards know that they were leaving. Jensen glanced back at Mr. Holland, who was trying to get Stacy to talk to him. It didn't look as though he was making any progress either.

When they reached the office upstairs, Jensen plopped down in her desk chair with exasperation.

"This is ridiculous. We should get a warrant and search Stacy's residence." Jensen suggested.

"You're right. I'll call Judge Cross." Dunn paced the office floor as he talked on the phone. From where Jensen was watching, it looked like it took a lot of convincing. Finally, Dunn walked back over to the desk.

"Our warrant will be ready in thirty minutes, but we have to find something, or this may be the last favor I get from Judge Cross." He sat down at his desk and started organizing it to pass the time. Jensen re-filled her coffee mug and started a new pot, then he sat down next to Dunn, sipping her coffee. They sat in silence for the next ten minutes, preparing for the task ahead.

Tracking down Stacy's home address had not been easy. She had no identification, no driver's license, and nothing was in her name. Dunn found an envelope in the pocket of Stacy's coat. The address on it was a P.O. Box. They had to get a release of records order signed by the judge to request the address Stacy used to apply for the box.

Stacy had been staying at a small cabin in the woods that belonged to her parents. Dunn and Jensen drove up the dusty dirt road in the unmarked cruiser. Dunn called Charlotte before he left and let her know where they would be.

"Will you please call and let us know what you find?" She asked. Dunn promised that he would.

The cabin looked abandoned. It was overgrown with ivy, which crept up the sides of the house. Jensen could tell that the landscape was once beautiful. Lilac bushes grew on the edges of the trees, and the fragrance seemed homey. The walkway leading to the steps was made from stone patio pavers and looked like a medieval castle floor. Dunn and Jensen walked cautiously to the door, which was slightly ajar. Dunn drew his weapon and pulled his flashlight off his holster. Dunn entered the room, making sure to perform a sweep of the corners. He found a light switch and tried to turn it on, but there was no power. As Jensen walked closer to the kitchen, a foul stench assaulted her nose. She could hear flies buzzing around the refrigerator. Jensen pulled her shirt up over her nose, took in a deep breath, held it, and then opened the fridge. Old and rotting food sat on the shelves growing green mold. Jensen closed the door quickly and ran from the room to take a breath of fresher air.

Dunn found a bedroom covered in a layer of dust and spider webs. He walked around, shining his light on the various trinkets and knickknacks meticulously arranged on the shelves that hung on every wall. A hinged photo frame sat on the chest of drawers with two photos in it. The people in the pictures looked old enough to be Stacy's parents. Dunn had found no death certificates for them during his online investigation, but if they were still alive, they had not been in this room for months by the looks of it.

Jensen worked her way past the kitchen to a door in the back. Around the frame of the door, Jensen noticed long strips of missing paint. Jensen expected to see a pantry behind that door, but instead, it revealed a staircase leading down. A musty stench rose from the basement. It was the unmistakable smell of decay-a smell that Jensen had never had the displeasure of smelling until they had found Verona's body. Jensen replaced her shirt over her nose and then cautiously stepped onto the first wooden step. It creaked loudly and bowed in the middle under her foot, and the next step was the same.

Dunn had moved on from the dust-covered bedroom and on to the next. This room was different from the last; there were no cobwebs or inch-thick layers of dust. The bed was left unmade, and the red mesh curtains were drawn, casting a sinister glow over the room. *Someone has used this room recently,* Dunn thought.

Dunn moved to the dresser and began going through the drawers. The top drawer contained bras and panties, mostly black with some red here and there. Dunn pulled out a leather corset and examined it. *Okay, interesting,* He thought as he dropped it back into the drawer. On top of the dresser, there was a small lock box. He tried to lift the lid, and to his surprise, it opened easily. Dunn pulled out a stack of photos, most of Stacy, wearing the leather corset with a black lace bra and matching panties. Dunn tried to recognize the familiar decor in the background of the pictures but was unable to.

Dunn took the photos, placed them in a plastic bag, then moved on to the closet. Dunn saw several holes in the door, the wood splintered outward. He opened it, and Verona stared back at him. The yearbook photo was blown up and pinned to the back of the door. Several long gouges in the photo-matching the fragments on the outside of the door- suggested that someone had been using the photo for throwing knife target practice. Dunn snapped a photo with his phone. As he closed the closet door, a blood-curdling scream came from another room.

"Jensen!" Dunn shouted. He ran through the dark cabin in the direction of the sound. Dunn bellowed her name again as he ran, knocking over several pieces of furniture that stood in his way. Yet another scream led him to the door to the basement. Dunn took the stairs two at a time. One of them snapped under his weight, and he stumbled to the concrete floor below. His flashlight spun around as it clattered to the floor and then halted on a badly decomposed corpse. Dunn gasped in shock as he rolled off his stomach and stumbled backward, trying desperately to get away from the corpse. He grabbed his flashlight as he backed away. He swept the light around the room until he spotted Jensen. She sat on the cement floor, hyperventilating, with yet another corpse a few feet in front of her.

# CHAPTER THIRTEEN

Grant was at his office, between patients when his secretary alerted him to an urgent call from the district attorney's office. He looked confused for a moment but then picked up the phone. The conversation was brief. They needed him to provide his medical opinion on Stacy Morris's mental state and her ability to stand trial. They knew that she had been a patient of his and asked for her file. They had a warrant that they would be presenting within the hour. Grant pulled her file and began reading over the session notes from the past year that she had been under his care.

*Major Depressive Disorder, Bipolar disorder, and Schizophrenia* were the diagnoses Grant had assigned to her over their sessions together. He had prescribed her medication, but the last time she came in for an appointment, it was clear she had stopped taking them. She had been angry and delusional that day. She had spent most of the session begging him not to break up with her, although there had never been any relationship, to begin with, aside from the doctor-patient relationship. That had also been the day Adam had come to confront him about his relationship with Verona. He had been honest with him. There was no reason to lie; the truth had been in her womb when she died.

Grant tried to push the thoughts of Verona out of his mind. He had been doing well lately, coping with her death and coping with the loss of their child, who never even got a chance to take their first breath.

Grant had his new secretary cancel the rest of his appointments for the day and then sent her home early.

"Don't worry; I'll pay you for the full day; go on, enjoy your family." He told her.

She thanked him as she grabbed her purse and jacket, leaving Grant to wait alone in an empty office. Charlotte had kept Grant informed on how the investigation was going. He knew about Stacy's attack on Charlotte to destroy the evidence she collected. Grant also knew that in addition to the assault, Dunn and Jensen thought that Stacy was also responsible for Verona's death, but they needed proof before charging her.

Mike Nicholson and Henry Bloom were the officers who came for Stacy's file. Grant handed it to Officer Bloom, and they turned to leave.

"Wait." Grant rushed across the room to catch them. "Can Stacy have visitors?" He asked.

Nicholson nodded. "Sure, Why?"

"I was her therapist; I just thought maybe she might be honest with me."

"Good luck; no one has been able to get her to talk. Today we had to put her on suicide watch. She isn't eating, and she keeps beating herself up, throwing herself around her cell," Nicholson said.

"I'll follow you. I want to try. I have to know if Stacy killed Verona."

Grant signed the visitor log, and the jailer buzzed him into the cell block. A beefy guard led him to the interview room, and two other guards brought Stacy in. Stacy was covered in cuts and bruises; he noticed large patches of hair missing from her head and scabs where her hair used to be. The dark, puffy circles under her eyes told Grant it had been some time since Stacy enjoyed a good night's sleep. The guards seated Stacy across from Grant, then cuffed her to the chair. When the guards exited, Grant continued to study Stacy for a moment before speaking.

"Stacy, can you tell me how you're feeling right now?" Grant asked.

Stacy started shaking her head from side to side.

"Why not? Are you afraid of someone here?" Grant ducked his head to try to meet her eye.

She moved her eyes away from Grant's and continued to shake her head. Grant decided to ask a question to which he already knew the answer.

"Did you assault Charlotte Bradley?"

She continued to shake her head. Her face seemed to contort as if she were in pain. Stacy closed her eyes as it looked like she was trying to talk, but her voice wouldn't work. She opened her eyes, and tears fell from them. Grant wanted to encourage her to speak, so he reached across the table and rested his hand on hers. His touch seemed to send a shock through her body, and she began to scream a monotone high-pitched screech that sounded almost demonic. He pulled his hand back quickly, startled by her response.

The interview room door burst open as the two guards that brought her rushed to grab her. One took off the cuffs, while the other helped her to her feet. As they took her from the room, she reached out her hand to Grant, her eyes were pleading, but she was still shaking her head.

"No! No! No!" She screamed, actual words as they took her from the room.

"Wait!" Grant tried to stop them, but the nurse rushed down the hall to meet them and pressed a needle into Stacy's arm. She pressed down on the plunger, emptying the syringe into the injection site. Grant showed himself out as they helped Stacy back to her cell. Grant slumped against the wall and buried his face in his hands, running his fingertips from his eyes, down his cheeks, his heart was pounding, and he was still half in shock from the scene he just witnessed.

"Do you have a doctor here or just the nurse?" He asked the guard behind the desk.

"Just the nurse."

"Do you get a medical history for your inmates, Thompson?" Grant asked, looking at the man's name tag. Thompson only looked confused.

"Look, I have been treating Stacy Morris for a year. She has Schizophrenia, among other things. She was on medication, and it is clear she hasn't been getting it, which I am sure is why she is in the state she is in now." Grant realized he was yelling and lowered his voice.

"You can always write her a prescription, and the nurse can fill it."

Grant pulled his prescription pad out of his messenger bag and began writing out Stacy's prescriptions for Clozapine and citalopram.

"This one is her anti-depressant. This one is her anti-psychotic. She needs them both daily, preferably with breakfast." Grant handed Thompson the prescriptions one at a time. Thompson called the nurse and gave them to her.

"I'm going to come back in a week if she is still here, and hopefully, we will see some improvement." Grant turned and walked toward the elevator, still unable to shake Stacy's strange behavior.

That night at home, Grant had turned on the television, hoping to numb his brain to the day's events. He was flipping through the channels when he stopped on the local news. Verona's parents were on the screen. Grant turned the volume up.

"Please, whoever took our daughter, we just want to know that she is okay. Milan is a wonderful daughter and friend. We miss her. She is my baby, and I just want her back." Mrs. Warren was pleading. *Is Milan missing now too?* Grant thought. *If Stacy is behind bars, these occurrences can't be related.*

Grant kept watching the Warrens take turns begging for the return of Milan. He walked to the liquor cabinet and poured a glass of whiskey. He drank it straight, hissing at the burn that followed. The news went on and moved to other stories as his whiskey bottle emptied a glass at a time. Grant was sitting in the recliner, and he started to nod off. The whiskey glass began to slip from his hand as his grip loosened. The movement jarred him, and he was able to catch the glass before it hit the floor. After setting the glass on the end table beside the recliner, he nodded off again.

Verona came to him in his dreams. Walking toward him with an outstretched arm, she was smiling. Grant saw that Verona's face was gray, bloody, and covered in dirt as she got closer to him. Her hand, which had been beckoning for him, twisted into a claw and grabbed for his throat. He felt himself choking, and his eyes snapped open, but he couldn't move. Fear paralyzed him and rooted him to the chair as the grip around his throat tightened. His eyes began to bulge as he felt the restriction of oxygen. The hand around his throat was no longer attached to Verona; the face he saw now was Stacy's.

A loud crash from outside startled Grant awake-really awake-this time. There was no hand around his throat, no Stacy, and no Verona. He tried to stand, but the room started spinning around him, and he went down again, this time, onto the sofa, which is where he woke up around noon the next day.

# CHAPTER FOURTEEN

The Ross Lake PD placed Dunn and Jensen on a mental health leave of absence following the incident at Stacy's parents' cabin. The stipulations of their return to duty included a psychological evaluation and a hundred and twenty hours of therapy. Of course, Dunn was thoroughly pissed off about this, insisting the whole time that he was "Just fine." and "Only snowflakes let a couple of dead bodies keep them from doing their job." His anger, which Dr. Green had said was all a part of the grieving process, kept him from progressing in his therapy. Dr. Green said they needed a breakthrough to help him let go of the anger and finally move on to the next step, which he knew, was bargaining.

"How's this for bargaining, Doc? You give me a clean bill of mental health, and I won't tell everyone what a quack you are. The grieving process, my ass. I didn't even know them." He huffed and crossed his arms, sitting on the leather chaise lounge in the psychiatrist's office.

"You know I can't do that. You could lose your job, and I could lose mine." Dr. Green wrote something down in her notebook.

"Why don't we talk about what happened at the cabin?" She prompted.

"Nothing to talk about, we searched a house and found a couple of bodies. It's all part of the job." Dunn seemed to believe that, but Dr. Green noticed a hint of fear in his eyes.

"Have you been getting eight hours of sleep each night?" Dr. Green asked. Dunn laughed.

"I haven't gotten eight hours of sleep a night since high school."

"How often do you wake during the night?" Dr. Green continued.

"Once to pee around three in the morning, and then when my alarm goes off at five." Dunn started to relax a little as his anger subsided.

"Well, we are almost out of time for today. Is there anything else you wanted to talk about before you leave?" Dr. Green closed her notebook and looked at him. Dunn shook his head and sat silently.

"Very well." She stood and showed Dunn to the door. "Today is Tuesday; how about you come back on Thursday. We can make this your regular schedule if you like."

"Sounds fine, not like I have a choice," Dunn grumbled under his breath, which Dr. Green chose to ignore.

"Great. See you Thursday."

Dunn drove around for a bit to clear his head. He loved driving up to the bluffs at Ross Lake for lunch and did so at least a few times each week when things were slow, but he hadn't been there now since they found Verona's body, so that is where he went. When Dunn got to the top, he noticed that someone had recently smashed through the guardrail separating the parking area from the lake below. Dunn hadn't heard about an accident, but maybe no one had been around when it happened.

Dunn pulled his car off the side of the road on the opposite side of the gravel parking area. He looked carefully for tire tracks and saw definite indentations in the gravel in front of where the guard rail used to be. The officer in him wanted to investigate, but the anger inside him screamed at him that it wasn't his problem-he was suspended. Dunn grabbed his phone and called it in.

An hour later, the lake was swarming with police. The officer in charge called in a dive team and a tow truck, the kind with the enormous hydraulic winch on the back. Divers dragged the winch line down into the lake with them. When they found the car, one of them attached the winch to the rear frame. It took about ten minutes, but finally, the divers emerged. Once they were safe on the shore, the tow truck operator turned on the winch. Twenty more minutes passed before the car broke the surface of the lake.

The operator worked the winch at a slow but steady pace because a vehicle that generally weighed four thousand pounds, filled with water, would easily double that weight, and reeling that much weight too quickly could damage the winch.

By the time the car was entirely on the shore, groups of people had gathered around trying to get a peek. A couple of officers were on 'crowd control' while the others taped off the area. Dunn recognized the car. He and Jensen had spent enough time parked behind it or tailing it. There was no mistaking that the vehicle belonged to Milan Warren.

The officer photographing the scene shouted to the others when he got to the driver's side.

"We got a body!" another officer rushed forward with gloved hands to open the driver's side door. He opened it slowly, and water gushed out, soaking his pants and shoes.

"Shit!" He shouted and let out a heavy sigh as the body slumped sideways and fell out of the car. They worked quickly to remove the body from the scene. Exposure to the air after drowning expedites decomposition, so everyone rushed to ensure examination within two hours of removal to minimize the risk of losing evidence. Dunn came forward to talk to the officer in charge.

"Call Madeline and Henry Warren. This body is their missing daughter." Dunn said. The officer turned and quickly delegated this task to another, then walked away from Dunn without another word.

Dunn felt helpless. If he weren't on suspension, this would be his crime scene and his call to make. He thought of the Warrens, how they were going to feel finding out that the only child they had left was gone, and how they were going to feel, hearing the news from a stranger who felt no empathy for them.

*Well, maybe he feels empathy, but he doesn't know them.* Dunn thought.


Dunn left the scene and drove home to his studio apartment. He ached to his bones and could think of nothing else at that moment besides his desire to forget the past few months. His bed beckoned him, and he obliged, falling into a deep, dreamless sleep.

# CHAPTER FIFTEEN

Stacy hated the way the old jail sounded at night; the echo of footsteps from passing guards, the whistle of the wind blowing down the hall when doors would open and close, and the loud screech the metal bars would sometimes make as the guards dragged the steel doors across their rails. There was a newer jail on the floor above them, but the crazies weren't allowed in gen-pop.

Stacy knew the things people were saying about her, they thought she wasn't listening because she wasn't talking, so they spoke freely in front of her. Stacy had to fight to stay conscious and in control, between the sedation and the voice in her head; it was a battle she rarely won. Stacy didn't understand what was happening, but it felt like sometimes she wasn't in charge of her body or her mind. The doctors said it was schizophrenia, but this was different; rather than feeling empty, Stacy felt filled up.

The bed in her cell looked more like a folding table that pulls down from the wall. It had a mattress on it that was just thick enough to be considered humane. The bathroom was a small metal toilet that flushed; thankfully, although the bowl never filled up with water, she also had a small metal sink for hand-washing. There was a leak in the pipe under the sink, and she counted the drips to try to sleep.

The nurse had been coming around and giving her medication. The pills dulled the voices in her head, all except the new one. The new voice just whispered one word. *Confess.* The voice seemed to grow impatient after speaking and would pull Stacy's body, throwing it against the wall. None of the other voices had ever hurt her, but she was afraid of this new one. In the last two days alone, she had been thrown against the wall repeatedly and had her head smashed on the wall and the floor. The voice wouldn't let her eat but instead kept screaming the one word.

Today was the first time in a long while that Stacy felt like herself. She remembered when it happened-the exact moment. The guard who likes to sit just at the corner of the hall watching videos on his phone at full volume had turned on the evening news. Stacy heard the headlining story from the reporter blaring down the hall.

"Ross Lake PD recovered the body of Milan Warren today. A dive team assisted in the removal of her vehicle from the lake. I'm here with Officer Cook of the Ross Lake PD. Officer Cook; what can you tell us about this situation?

"All I can say is that we are currently investigating, and any-thing we find we will release to the public once the case is closed."

That was when it happened. Stacy felt empty again, like the voice inside her head went to sleep. At one point, Milan had been a good friend of hers, but even knowing that she died could not fill the emptiness with sadness. She felt relieved.

Stacy didn't remember why she was there in jail; she lost time and woke up in strange places over the last few weeks. The voice in her head kept telling her to confess; she had no memory of what she needed to confess. Stacy put it out of her mind; for now, the voice was quiet, which meant she could sleep.

Stacy awakened when the nurse came to hand out medica-tion. The nurse watched her take it and then asked to see the inside of her mouth. When she was satisfied that the pills were gone, she pushed her cart to the next cell. Stacy laid down again and went back to sleep.

*When she opened her eyes, she saw herself; her consciousness was outside her body. She was dirty and wet. Stacy watched herself stumble down the street and to a cheap motel. She stripped her clothes off, showered, and then under cover of night and wearing the white hotel robe, she deposited her clothing in the dumpster. Stacy walked to her mom and dad's cabin and went to sleep in her bed.*

*Stacy felt confused. She had no memory of this, but before she had the chance to process it, she felt a sickening crack on the back of her head. Her body dropped, and she caught a glimpse of the burning baseball bat that hit her. The bat burned and the ashes scattered to the wind in front of her. What was this dream trying to tell her?*

Her eyes jerked open and rage coursed through her body. She felt full again. She tried to fight it. Her brain screamed; *Get out! Get out!* She felt her body fly across the cell and slam against the wall. Her back cracked as her spine met with concrete. She hovered six inches off the floor with her back pressed to the wall. She was choking; she couldn't breathe. It had her by the throat. *CONFESS!* The voice screeched in her head. It was deafening, her ears continued to ring, and her head felt like it would explode.

Stacy could feel her eyes bulging out from lack of oxygen, and suddenly she flew across the cell again and her face smacked into the bars. The lights overhead flickered, and one by one popped as the bulbs shattered to the floor. Guards came running, having no idea what was going on. They found Stacy slumped on the floor, crying and bleeding. Her hair was matted with blood, and her face was red from her nose to her chin.

Officer Holland called an ambulance while Thompson called it in over the radio. Two officers arrived from upstairs to escort Stacy upstairs to the paramedics. Stacy's head was swimming, but the voice wasn't there. Everything went black as the sirens wailed and the ambulance rushed through town to the hospital.

# CHAPTER SIXTEEN

Sara Jensen was making significant progress with therapy. She had been going twice a week and had never felt better. The dimly lit office and welcoming decor made it easy to be comfortable. Sara had talked to Dr. Green about seeing her first body, the what happened in the Morris family cellar, she even spoke about her relationship with James. She had been nervous to talk about him because even though he was not a suspect, they had still interviewed him for a possible connection to Verona. After her fourth session, Dr. Green deemed her fit to return to duty as long as she continued her therapy.

On her first day back, a call came in for an escort to the hospital for Stacy Morris. Of course, she jumped at the chance to get back on the case, and so did Nolan Mayer. Nolan was the only other female officer in the department, other than the dispatcher, but she didn't leave the office anymore. Officer Mayer looked like she belonged on one of those popular crime shows on TV. Mayer had long blonde hair tied into a low bun so that it was both off her collar and low enough for her hat to rest comfortably in place. She was thin but muscular, an Army veteran, and tough as nails. She and her wife had just adopted a baby boy and often raised money and donated to different children's charities.

"Looks like I'm with you," Mayer said as she approached. "This was your case; I'll follow your lead."

Jensen smiled, but on the inside, she was squealing and doing a happy dance. "Okay, let's head to the hospital. The ambulance is leaving now." Jensen led the way to the patrol car she and Dunn used.

Jensen flipped on the lights and siren, which significantly reduced the time it took them to reach the hospital. They arrived just before the ambulance and had time to park as the ambulance's paramedics unloaded Stacy.

"She is unresponsive." The paramedic stated as a doctor and nurses rushed to the side of the gurney to assess. They quickly wheeled her out of sight before Jensen had a chance to speak or follow. A remaining nurse showed them to the waiting area beside the operating rooms.

"You can wait here. Do you need anything? Coffee? Water?" He asked, looking from Jensen to Mayer. They both politely declined and sat down in the barely comfortable chairs to wait. The time seemed to pass slowly, and when the Doctor did come out to greet them, it had been an hour, although it had felt like double that.

"Hello, I'm Doctor Phillips; I am caring for Stacy Morris." Dr. Phillips moved toward them with his hand outstretched. Jensen and Mayer both stood and took his hand. "Ms. Morris is in a coma. Her head injury is cleaned up and stitched, she has some broken ribs and was bleeding internally, but we could stop that. She has bruises around her neck as if someone grabbed her by the throat. These injuries seem fresh. I would launch an internal investigation if I were you and find out what happened. We are going to monitor her closely, and we will call you directly if her situation changes." Jensen and Mayer exchanged a look of equal parts of fear and confusion.

"We will, Thank you, Doctor. We want to go back and see her if it's okay. She is still a suspect in more than one murder case, so we need to make sure to cuff her hands to the bed rails. I am sure you understand." Jensen said.

"Sure." Dr. Phillips replied, but his face told Jensen that he was not a fan of the idea. Begrudgingly, he led them to Stacy's room. Jensen cuffed one wrist, while Mayer cuffed the other. They both looked at Stacy's bruises and then at each other. Jensen pulled out her phone and took pictures of the bruises around Stacy's neck. Mayer called for the nurse and asked her for a copy of Stacy's chart.

With all of the information and evidence they needed, Jensen and Mayer took their findings to the Ross Lake internal affairs office to file their official complaint. Jensen hated to think that someone in their department would treat a prisoner this way. She always did see the best in people, but this evidence was impossible to ignore.

"I'm going to get the video from the security cameras in and around Stacy's cell. Can you sign us into one of the AV rooms? Jensen asked Mayer.

An hour later, they watched the most disturbing video they had ever seen. Neither Mayer nor Jensen could explain what happened, how Stacy Morris levitated half a foot off the floor, or how her body flew from one side of her cell to the other. No one else entered her cell until the guards found her crumpled on the floor. The lights flashed like a strobe, making the video look like an old horror film. The time stamp on the video did not seem altered. There was nothing to suggest that the video was fake.

"I think what we need is an exorcist," Mayer said. Jensen couldn't tell if she was joking; or not, but her gut told her that she probably wasn't.

# CHAPTER SEVENTEEN

Adam was drunk again. This was becoming a regular occurrence. He hadn't recovered from the loss of Verona and was now coping with the loss of Milan. The investigators ruled it a suicide. There was no evidence to the contrary, so case-closed. *Case closed, and bottoms up* Adam thought as he tipped back the bottle and took a big gulp. His house was quiet, no more strange noises, no more flickering lights, just silence and a bottle of Tito's. Adam had to admit that he was powerless. Stacy Morris had been arrested for the assault on the private investigator that Dr. Hudson hired, but there was no proof that she killed Verona, although that's what the police suspected. Officer Jensen had come around with her new partner asking questions about Milan and even though he knew he didn't kill her, he felt no less responsible for her death. *If only I had answered my phone.* He thought.

Adam tipped the bottle back again, draining the last few drops out of it. He threw away the empty bottle and grabbed his jacket. He wasn't nearly drunk enough to forget his worries and there wasn't a drop of liquor left in the house. He took off walking down the street, to the bar on the corner a few blocks down. Although not drunk enough to forget, he knew he was far too drunk to drive. He sat down at the bar and ordered their cheapest whiskey and a diet soda. He was oblivious to the other patrons until one of them approached.

"Can I sit with you?" Grant asked.

Adam looked up in surprise. "Dr. Hudson, of course." He motioned to the empty stool next to him.

"Please, Adam, You can call me Grant." He took a long sip of his drink after he sat down next to Adam. The two of them drank together in silence for a while, each knowing the other's pain.

"I want you to know, I don't hold anything against you. I was a lousy husband, and Verona was so easy to love." Adam said.

Grant nodded. "That she was." They both took a drink.

"I was sorry to hear about Milan. I never spent a lot of time with her, but I imagine you knew her pretty well." Grant said, not knowing the full extent of the relationship between Adam and Milan.

"That I did." Adam nodded and then cracked a grin.

"I see what you did there!"

Grant and Adam drank and talked more, then they played pool and darts. In another life, one where Grant hadn't slept with his wife, Adam could see them being friends. Real friends, not whatever this was; It was nice, but if Verona was still alive, it never would have happened.

"Excuse me for a moment," Grant said as he spotted Charlotte across the bar. He waved to her as he walked over to greet her.

"You made it!" Grant called to her.

"I did! I brought Kristofer along, I hope you don't mind." She said.

"Of course not! The more the merrier. Have you met Adam?" Grant asked as they walked back over to where Adam was.

"I don't think we have, not officially. Hi, I'm Charlotte." She said.

Adam took her hand. "Nice to meet you, I'm Adam. I heard about what happened with Stacy. You doing okay?" Charlotte nodded.

"Let's get you a drink," Grant suggested. They moved to the bar, leaving Kristofer and Adam to make their introductions. The evening had a strange feel to it. Adam had never really had a group of friends before. His life had been about school, then work. He never focused on much else, not even his marriage, he was sad to admit.

A clap on his shoulder brought him out of his thoughts. "Want to play another round?" Grant asked motioning to the pool table. "We can play doubles." He hands Charlotte a cue and nods to the rack right behind Kristofer. "You and me, against Charlotte and Kristofer?" Grant suggested.

"Okay, but you rack 'em!" Charlotte teased.

When Adam awoke the next morning, his head was pounding. Despite the headache, Adam couldn't remember a time when he had as much fun as he did last night. He had almost forgotten about all the things weighing on him lately. Adam rubbed his eyes as they adjusted to the late morning sun peeking through the blinds in his bedroom window and he headed to the kitchen to put on a pot of coffee. Adam was thankful to have taken his vacation from work, there was no way he would be able to focus today.

After coffee, and packing a breakfast, Adam took a drive out to the lake. He ate his breakfast at the picnic table on the beach. He came to feel close to Milan, to try and understand why she would take such a drastic measure. He closed his eyes and felt the breeze on his face, it was the cool breeze of winter creeping in as autumn drifted off to sleep. The leaves were thick on the ground, and the trees nearly bare, yet a few ravens remained, squawking in the branches overhead, begging for the scraps of Adam's breakfast.

# CHAPTER EIGHTEEN

When Sara woke, she opened her eyes to see James smiling at her. She had no idea how long he had been watching her sleep, and it made her cheeks turn bright pink.

"Good morning to you too." She said as she pulled him in again.

"I thought we could go to brunch today, then spend the day together," James told her.

"I'm sorry I can't. I have to go to the hospital to check on Stacy. Then I have a meeting I have to go to. My partner, Dunn, is coming back today, and I have to fill him in." Sara said.

James's face fell, and he puffed out his bottom lip, looking at Sara with his puppy dog eyes.

Sara laughed. "I'll make it up to you, promise." She kissed him again, then got out of bed and began dressing. James followed suit.

"At least have a cup of coffee before you go. I'll go put on a pot right now." James said as he headed for the kitchen. Sara grabbed her toothbrush case out of her purse and performed her morning hygiene practices before joining James in the kitchen.

James held up a travel mug. "This way, if you don't finish it, you can take it with you." He smiled as he filled up her cup and finished it off with peppermint mocha creamer.

"What would I do without you?" Sara asked as James offered it to her.


When Jensen arrived at the hospital, Dunn was waiting for her.

"Hey there, partner!" He called.

Jensen hugged him. "I'm so glad you're back. It hasn't been the same without you."

They walked to Stacy's room and stopped short in the doorway. The curtain was drawn.

"Excuse me," Jensen turned toward the nurse who was sitting at the nurse's station, "Is she being examined?" The nurse looked confused.

"No, why?" She asked.

"The curtain is pulled."

The nurse got up from her chair and walked into Stacy's room. A scratching sound was coming from behind the curtains. She threw back the curtain as quickly as she could, and suddenly the room filled with a terrified scream. Stacy was facing the wall, digging her fingernails into it, leaving behind one bloody word. *Confess* was scratched into the wall over fifty times, and Stacy's fingers were covered in blood.

"Stacy!" Jensen shouted as she ran up to her. Just as she reached out to touch her shoulder, Stacy turned around and shrieked at Jensen. Stacy's eyes were completely black, and her face was twisted up in some inhuman form. Stacy grabbed Jensen by the shoulders and screamed again, breathing a vile hot stench into her face; then, both Stacy and Jensen collapsed to the floor.

Dunn rushed over to Jensen and sat her up. Her eyes fluttered open, and her pupils seemed to go from extremely large back to average size as her eyes adjusted to the light again.

"Are you okay?" He asked.

Jensen nodded and got to her feet. Stacy was still on the floor in front of her. The nurse ran over to her and picked her up. She began taking her vitals and lifting her eyelids to look at her pupils, which seemed to look normal again. Still, she remained unconscious, though. The nurse lifted Stacy and put her back into bed, then called for a doctor. The nurse reconnected the machines to Stacy, and she had to run a new IV because Stacy had ripped her old one out.

"I'm sorry, please excuse us; we need to let the doctor examine her." The nurse said as Dr. Phillips walked in.

"May we photograph her hands first?" Jensen asked. "You know before you clean her up." She added.

"Let me check her condition first, then you can come back in to take pictures. She is my priority, I am sure you understand." Dr. Phillips led them to the door, and with no other choice, they both nodded and retreated to the waiting room.

As promised, Stacy was just as she was when they left. "What happened to her?" Dunn asked the doctor.

"I'm honestly, not sure. Stacy is in a coma again, like she had never even come out of it." Dr. Phillips looked disturbed by the gouges in the wall. "It's hard to believe she did this with her fingernails. I would say she is wrestling with some guilt. I'm going to call Dr. Hudson. He is listed as her psychiatrist in her file." He ran his fingers over the word. *Confess.*

# CHAPTER NINETEEN

Stacy had not remembered dreaming for many years. She knew that everyone dreamed every night, but hers were forgotten every morning when she opened her eyes until now. The hour-long nap Stacy just woke up from had brought the most vivid dream she had ever had. It was a dream about the past, and she wouldn't have known it was a dream at all if not for the little differences and inconsistencies. Faces looked blurred, places looked backward, and small details were missing. *The Devil is in the details.* Stacy thought.

Being in the hospital was boring. They had said they wanted to keep Stacy overnight for observation, but she heard the doctor talking about transferring her to A1. Stacy knew that was the psych ward; she had been there before. She was still cuffed to the bed, and there was nothing she cared to watch on the television. Stacy closed her eyes and drifted off to sleep again. Once more, a dream swept her away where she could be free.

*Stacy walked the familiar hall of Ross Lake High. The rows of red lockers seemed never-ending as the corridor stretched before her. She began to run through the long hall; no matter how long and far she ran, the hall stayed the same, extending into the distance before her. She turned back and ran in the direction from which she had come. At the end of this hall stood a figure. Stacy couldn't make out what it was. It had grown dark.*

*The hall was filled with a deafening scream followed by silence. The shadow began to walk out the front doors and down the street, where it disappeared around the corner. Stacy ran after it. Just as she rounded the corner, she came face to face with Verona, and the scenery changed. Stacy was at Verona's house; Verona was braiding her hair. Roman brought them hot cocoa and popcorn. He turned on a movie for them and left the room. They drank their cocoa, laughed, played truth or dare, and talked about the boys they liked.*

*The world shifted, blurred, and melted away. The scene completely changed, taking the people with it. Stacy was standing by Verona's side with Milan on the other side of her as they cried. A hole in front of them beckoned her to look closer. She stepped forward slowly. She knew this was when she had gone to Roman's funeral. They had each thrown in a rose before the caretaker began shoveling dirt on top of the casket. Stacy walked forward as the voice whispered to her. She was close enough to peer into the hole now, and she could hear the whisper clearly and make out what it was saying. "Confess," it said, "Confess." a hand clawed its way up out of the fresh dirt and grabbed Stacy by the throat. Verona's face rose from the grave, attached to the hand that was squeezing the life out of her. A silky black veil poured over the scene like the opposite of spilled milk.*

*Stacy was now at homecoming. She was dancing with Adam. She looked at Verona, and out of spite, grabbed Adam and pressed her lips to his. He pushed her away, but it was too late. The damage was already done. 'That will teach her to steal my boyfriend.' She remembered the thought going through her head as she watched Verona flee from the gymnasium in tears. Stacy also remembered how it felt when Adam shot her that hateful glance and took off after Verona. That night she had taped Verona's yearbook picture to her closet door and threw her father's pocket knife at it until she felt better. Now she was alone in her room trying to sleep, and there was a pounding on her door. It swung open; it was Henry. "CONFESS!" He screamed at her and then came the bat, everything went black.*

*Next, she saw Henry tied to the chair in his study as she danced around in her lingerie in front of him. The door burst open, and Verona began shouting at the both of them. Henry broke out of the loose bonds that only pretended to hold him and stood up, fumbling to quickly pull up his pants.*

*"I'm texting mom right now," Verona told him, and then she snapped pictures. Stacy saw the dread on his face, and he rushed across the room. Henry tried to wrestle the phone from Verona, but she rammed her knee into his groin. He howled in pain but*

*managed to get the phone. Verona rushed him like a bull, pushing him back. Henry fell into his chair, and Just as Verona wrestled the phone out of her father's hand, Stacy hit her over the head with the autographed baseball bat that Henry had mounted to his office wall.*

Stacy woke up unable to breathe and looked around, expecting to see her bedroom in the cabin, with its red glow, but it was the hospital room that came into focus. She remembered everything.

# CHAPTER TWENTY

Charlotte had hit a wall. She didn't know where to go from here, how to proceed. Charlotte felt like there had to be something she missed. Charlotte pulled out her file on the case and began looking back through her notes and photos. *Maybe it's time.* She thought she had only said the words in her mind, but Kristofer replied from across the room.

"Time for what?"

"Time for me to admit that this case has gone cold and to see if Dunn and Jensen have any more leads. I haven't had a chance to talk to them since the day at the cabin; I'm not even sure what they found."

"Let's set up a meeting; four minds are better than two." Kristofer raised his eyebrows at his sister. "Right?"

"Yeah, okay." Charlotte pulled out her phone and called Dunn.

They met at a coffee shop a mile from the hotel. A genius place to assemble, too, at least Charlotte thought so because she had not yet had her morning cup of coffee. Dunn and Jensen were off duty, so they did not come in uniform. Charlotte almost didn't recognize them until Jensen waved to her from across the room.

"Harry, Sara, so nice to see you both!" Charlotte stood to greet them. They each wrapped her in a hug before sitting down at the table. Dunn set his briefcase on the table and slid it across the table to Charlotte.

"This is everything we have so far. The manila envelope has photos from Stacy's room in the cabin. They're, uh, a little racy." He cleared his throat. Charlotte grabbed the envelope first. She pulled out the photos, and her eyes widened.

"No way!" Charlotte exclaimed. "I know where these photos were taken." She pulled out her own folder of photos printed from her phone and showed Dunn the picture of Henry Warren and the mystery girl she now knew was Stacy.

"We need to talk to Mr. Warren. If we come at him with what we know, he is guaranteed to lawyer up. We have to have a plan." Charlotte suggested.

"We could just ask him about Stacy's friendship with his daughters, don't let him know that we even suspect anything between him and Stacy," Jensen said.

"The problem with that is, He likely has heard about Stacy's condition; if he knows she can't talk, then Henry could say whatever he wants, thinking we have no proof of anything without her testimony. "Dunn shuffled the photos and put them back into the folder. "I say, we plant a little rumor that Stacy woke up and is talking. Then we wait. He is likely to try to visit her to make sure she keeps their secret." Dunn looked at the others. Before anyone had a chance to respond, Jensen's phone rang.

"It's Dr. Phillips," Jensen said as she quickly took the call. Dunn, Charlotte, and Kristofer listened to one end of the conversation until Jensen hung up the phone. They looked at her with anticipation.

"Well, is she awake?" Kristofer asked.

"No, but they have been running her labs. She had several drugs in her system, a small amount since she has been in custody, but they think her condition is caused by the damage these drugs have done to her brain. Apparently, she has been an addict for a long time. Stacy has been using heroin in addition to her prescriptions. I am sure if Grant knew about her drug problem, he never would have prescribed what he did." Jensen explained.

"You're probably right, but it couldn't hurt to ask him," Dunn said. "Let's get some more coffee for the road and then head out. Charlotte, you guys coming?"

"Absolutely." Charlotte gathered her things and went to the coffee counter to order. When she got her cup, she immediately looked at the name scribbled on it by the young barista; *Shirley? Why can't they ever get it right?* She chuckled to herself and sighed as she took a small sip. When Kristofer had his coffee, Charlotte turned to Dunn, who was still in line. "We will meet you there." Dunn nodded and waved.

Grant was surprised to see the four of them when they arrived, but he was pleased, and he welcomed them in.

"Not at the office today?" Dunn asked.

"No, this is the one day a week I spend typing up my case notes and transcribing my sessions from the week," Grant explained as he gestured to his open laptop on the desk. He had a nice pair of noise-canceling headphones, the wireless kind, and a coffee mug beside his computer.

"We had a few questions about Stacy's medications. Her doctor seems to think that her brain has been damaged by combining the drug you prescribed and the heroin she was using. Did you know she was an addict?" Jensen asked.

"I knew she had trouble with drugs in the past. First, it was pain pills, then other things; when she came back to my office and asked for medication, I made her take a drug test. I asked her to come in every week and test clean for three weeks before giving her any new medications. If she began using again after I prescribed to her, I couldn't say, but a clean test was required for each month's prescription." Grant said. "I can pull up her case file now, and you can have a look. She tested clean for six months straight." Grant moved to the computer and began searching Stacy's name in his file folder.

"It's okay; we believe you," Dunn said.

Grant sighed in relief. "Thank you. How is Stacy, by the way? I heard about her episode."

"She is in a coma but having episodes of this dreamlike state where her pupils are completely dilated and dominating her eyes. Well- one episode so far, but still, it was scary." Jensen told him.

"Sounds like it." Grant agreed.

Jensen's skin began to itch, and she felt hot. She looked at Grant and suddenly felt drawn to him; she wanted to kiss him, hold him, and jump into his arms. When she realized this strange sensation, she tried to shake herself out of it. She excused herself and found the bathroom, splashing cold water in her face. She looked in the mirror and noticed her eyes looked different, her pupils were enlarged, and the whites were bloodshot. *Maybe I am exhausted.* She thought.

Jensen joined the others once more to explain that she wasn't feeling well and needed some air.

"Want me to drive you home?" Dunn offered.

"No, thank you though, I'm just going to take a walk," Jensen said.


Jensen walked and walked for a long time, not knowing where she was going; it was like someone else was guiding her steps and her direction. She walked past Adam's, pausing briefly to notice that the lights inside were on, and Adam's shadow paced back and forth across the living room. She felt herself being pulled away. Sara started walking again, letting the gentle tug move her body in the direction it wanted to go. She felt like she was destined to follow this path; this entity or feeling- whatever this was- would lead her to something she was meant to see.

Her path led to Henry and Madeline's house. There was a light on in one room, but the rest of the house was dark. She felt herself being drawn in by the large porch and then the door; before she knew what was happening, she was reaching for the handle. She tried to fight back. She tried to stop herself, but whatever was controlling her was overpowering, and her hand shot forward, grasping the handle. Her knuckles turned white as she tried to remove her hand, but the door pushed open, and then she stood in the foyer.

Jensen walked down the hall to Henry's office. She felt herself crying deep inside herself, knowing she was unable to take control. *Please, No, don't make me do this.* Jensen begged, feeling the anger that wasn't her own. Henry was sitting at his desk, typing on his laptop. He jumped up out of his seat, knocking it over as he backed away.

"How the hell did you get in here? Why are you here?" He screamed at her. Jensen couldn't answer, but she heard the word leave her mouth. "CONFESS!" The voice was guttural and not her own; she wasn't even sure it was entirely human. Henry looked at her in shock, he backed away with apparent fear in his eyes, and again the voice rose from her and demanded him to confess.

Jensen tried to fight back against the urge to lunge forward and grab him by the throat. Jensen screamed for it to stop, but the words did not pass her lips. Henry reached the bookshelf and pulled out an encyclopedia. He opened it quickly and pulled a gun out of the hollowed shell of the book. The voice that wasn't hers shrieked again. "CONFESS!" Henry raised the gun, took aim, and as he discharged the weapon, a sickening crack erupted from Jensen's body as she quickly crumpled to the floor and out of the path of the bullet.

She couldn't fight it. Jensen lunged at Henry, grabbing him by the throat. Her mouth opened as she screeched at him. Jensen felt herself coming back as the monotone shriek continued, and a thick black smoke drifted from her mouth and into Henry's. When She felt in control again, she released Henry, but his eyes turned black, and he slumped down against the bookshelf, too weak to stand anymore. Henry began whispering, low and raspy.

"Confess, confess, confess," he whispered.

Jensen turned and ran from the house. How would she tell anyone what happened here? Jensen called Dunn when she was safely outside on the porch and spent the ten minutes it took him to arrive, pacing and dreading telling him what happened. *What if he doesn't believe me? What if Dunn thinks I'm crazy?*

*What if he thinks it's the job and that I can't handle it.* Her thoughts raced, and she bit her nails as she paced and waited.

"What happened?" Dunn asked as he got out of his car and ran to his partner. "Sara, are you okay? Did he hurt you?" His tone became more urgent.

"No, but I have to show you something. We need to go back to the station, but if we leave Henry here, I'm not sure what might happen to him. She said.

Dunn looked at her with confusion. "What are you talking about?"

"I will show you when we get to the station, but we have to take Henry with us," Jensen said.

Dunn did as requested. He put Henry Warren into the back of his car, and Jensen took her seat in the front. Jensen looked back at Henry. She was nervous about what he would say. *Will he tell Dunn that I broke into his house? Will he say that I attacked him?"* When they got to the station, Jensen locked Henry in one of the holding cells. She got the DVD of the hospital footage from evidence and played it on her computer for Dunn.

"I know what is happening here, and before I say it, I want you to know that I am not crazy, despite how this may sound. Stop smiling; it's not funny." Dunn had given her a smirk as soon as she said she wasn't crazy, and of course, he couldn't resist trying to lighten the mood.

"She's possessed," Jensen said.

"She's what now?" Dunn looked at her in shock.

"Possessed," Jensen repeated.

"There is no such thing," Dunn said in disbelief.

"I used to think so too, but I felt it, some being inside me, moving my body for me tonight when I ended up at Mr. Warren's. *It* took me there because it wanted Henry. It kept screaming *Confess.*" Jensen explained. Just then, her phone rang, startling her.

"Hello... Yes. Okay. Thank you, we will be right there." Jensen hung up and looked at Dunn, who was watching her with anticipation.

"It's Dr. Phillips. Stacy is awake and doing well. She might be able to give a statement." Jensen turned off the video, and Dunn began gathering his things, still unable to process what he had seen on the video and what Jensen told him.

When Dunn and Jensen arrived at Stacy's room, she was sitting up in her bed with her lunch tray in front of her. She was eating as though she had never seen a meal in her life and barely looked up from her plate when they entered.

"We will let you finish. Can we get you some more? Are you still hungry?" Jensen asked.

Stacy nodded and looked like she would have spoken had her mouth not been full. Jensen went into the hallway and asked the nurse at the station if it was too late to order another tray. Luckily, it wasn't, and Jensen ordered another of whatever meal Stacy had just devoured, then went back into the room. She looked at

Stacy, who now had color in her cheeks. Her blond bob was a tangled mess from bedhead and probably from wrestling with whatever, or whoever it was that wanted her to confess.

"I'm glad to see you're feeling better," Jensen told her with a smile.

"Thanks, me too." Stacy's words sounded clear-headed.

"Can you tell us about how you have been feeling lately? We have seen some pretty scary episodes, any ideas?" Jensen prompted.

"I wasn't myself. Dr. Hudson says I have schizophrenia, so I hear voices, and sometimes, I lose time." Stacy explained.

"What do you mean, *lose time*?" Dunn asked.

"Like, I wake up in strange places, not knowing how I got there, or I do things I have no memory of." Stacy looked away.

"That sounds like more than schizophrenia. I'm no Psychiatrist, though." Jensen said.

"Any idea what this is about?" Dunn gestured to the wall, where Stacy had scratched the word 'confess' into it several times. Stacy looked at the writings then looked back at Dunn and Jensen but didn't speak.

"What about Charlotte Bradley? She was assaulted at the gas station." Jensen asked.

"I saw her and that guy she was with sitting outside Adam's house. They were watching him, so I watched them. I followed them out to James Alden's Uncle's place, and I had to find out what they knew. When they stopped at the gas station, I followed Charlotte in. I saw her go to the bathroom. I went too. I got in the stall next to hers and waited for her to walk out. I had my stainless steel water bottle with me, so I bashed her with it. I grabbed her phone, and luckily, it was still unlocked. I guess she was using it in the bathroom. I thought maybe she had been taking pictures of Adam, so I looked through her pictures. I was surprised to see that she had a photo of Adam and me, and James and Verona. I deleted her evidence and walked out as if nothing happened." She started crying.

"We found your parents. Want to talk about them?"

Stacy's face turned angry as she narrowed her eyes and furrowed her brow at Jensen. She shook her head.

"What about Henry Warren?" Jensen asked as she studied Stacy's face for a reaction. She looked afraid and surprised. "Is there something you need to confess that involves him?" Stacy shut down. She crossed her arms and sat staring, her expression unchanged.

"I don't want to talk about him either." She said and then was silent again, looking through the window and getting lost in the open space. Jensen knew this was the last they were going to hear from her right now.

Dunn and Jensen excused themselves and didn't talk until they were safely back in the cruiser.

"I think we should play them against each other. Let's talk to Henry and tell him Stacy already told us everything." Jensen suggested.

"That might not be a bad idea, only, we don't know what state Henry will be in when we return," Dunn said as he pulled out of the hospital parking lot.

# CHAPTER TWENTY-ONE

The weeks passed, and the winter winds came, covering everything in a blanket of fresh snow. The investigation slowed due to the lack of tangible evidence. The judge and jury would laugh their tale of possession and ghosts out of the courtroom. With no confession, no murder weapon, and several motives, a prosecution would be impossible. Jensen knew they needed more evidence, but how? Henry refused to talk and called a lawyer, who advised him to keep quiet, knowing that the police had nothing. Stacy was not talking anymore either and was currently committed and not allowed visitors. Jensen wasn't sure if this was a hospital rule or a request from Stacy. Verona's case got put on the back burner while Jensen and Dunn worked on other cases; the most recent of them was Stacy's parents' mysterious death. The medical examiner couldn't determine the cause of death, just that Mrs. Morris suffered a broken neck and a fractured leg. Their death was labeled suspicious.

When Jensen clocked out, she found James waiting for her in the parking lot. James had slicked back his dark hair and his eyes, even in the darkness, were cool and blue like the Caribbean. He smiled when he saw her crossing the parking lot, and she ran into his open arms.

"I thought since you were off for the weekend, we could go somewhere," James said.

"Where?" Sara smiled at him, feeling lost in his eyes.

"I had a few places in mind, Vegas, Niagara Falls, The Grand Canyon, Mexico; take your pick."

"I have always wanted to go to Vegas! We could see some shows, and play poker, maybe even try our luck at the slot machines." Sara said.

"It's settled then. I'll drive you home so you can pack a bag. I'll buy the tickets while you're packing. I'm packed and ready." He gestured to his suitcase in the backseat. Sara got into his car with a squeal of excitement. In no time at all, they were in the air on their way to Vegas.


Grant came to terms with the lack of evidence in Verona's case and paid Charlotte what she was due. She moved on to other cases but kept in touch with Grant as if they were old friends. Grant focused on his work and helping as many people as he could. He thought of Stacy often and wished that he could still be her doctor. He was sure that she was involved in Verona's death but couldn't prove it. Grant had been spending a lot of time with Adam, they had become good friends lately, and it was a welcome change. Adam seemed to be healing, getting over the loss of Verona and Milan. He was even dating again. Adam had introduced Grant to his new girlfriend, Riley, over drinks. She brought a friend so Grant wouldn't feel like a third wheel.

"Hi, I'm Iris." Riley's friend extended her hand to Grant. Iris's emerald eyes sparkled as she felt his hand in hers.

"I'm Grant; nice to meet you." He caught himself staring; she was beautiful. Her hair was strawberry blonde and flowed in loose curls to her waist. Her cheeks were very lightly freckled, and the freckles were spread thin and lightly across her button nose. Her smile was bright and beautiful, and she seemed to radiate happiness. Whether or not Grant was ready to date, one thing was sure; he could use a little pleasure in his life. They spent the evening getting to know one another by the bar, and when the band began playing, she pulled him to the dance floor. Adam smiled as he watched them and looked over at Riley.

"I think you did a good job setting him up." He told her. "Look how happy he looks."

"I think it's sweet that you care so much about your friends. Your wife was a lucky woman." Adam winced. He had told her that his wife had passed; he neglected to mention the details surrounding her death. He also forgot to mention how he failed as a husband while she was alive.

"She wasn't. I wasn't a perfect husband. I worked all the time; I never came home. She deserved better, and I wish I had given her what she needed. Let's just say that I have learned from my mistakes, though, and change the subject, please. I didn't mean to kill the mood but had to clear the air."

"Your honesty is inspiring, but yes, I agree. Let's change the subject." She rose to her feet and extended a hand to Adam, asking him to dance. Adam followed her to the dance floor just as the music changed from an upbeat hip hop song to a slow, classical-inspired love song. Adam took her in his arms and held her against his chest. He saw Grant and Iris in the middle of the room. They looked like they were on an episode of *Dancing With the Stars* the way they elegantly waltzed across the floor. The other dancers began to back up, making room for them to move freely. Grant delicately twirled Iris into him, holding her back to his chest for a moment, and his lips brushed her jawline before he slowly spun her out again. Their dance ended with an extravagant dip with Iris's leg level to Grant's hip. Their audience burst into applause as she curtsied, and he took a bow. They joined Adam and Riley back at the table, out of breath and exhilarated.

"That was amazing! Where did you learn to dance like that?" Riley asked.

"I was forced to take ballroom dancing classes at my boarding school in England," Grant said.

"I took ballet and ballroom dancing since I was three," Iris said. She smiled at Grant, and for the first time in a very long time, he felt happy. When the night was over, Grant drove Iris home and walked her to her door, not wanting the night to end.

"I had a really amazing time with you." She said, looking up at him with her emerald eyes.

"I did too." He smiled at her and tucked a strand of hair behind her ear.

"I don't mean to be too forward, but I would like to kiss you. May I?" Grant asked.

Iris's heart fluttered, and she nodded as she stepped closer. He leaned in and pressed his lips to hers gently as he caressed her jaw with his hand. Iris deepened the kiss, and when they released each other, they were both breathless.

"Call me?" She whispered, nuzzling his neck.

"Is tomorrow too soon?"

"Not soon enough," Iris said, and she kissed him again.

# CHAPTER TWENTY-TWO

Ross Lake PD released Henry Warren. They didn't have enough to hold him. Dunn put a tail on him and had his phone monitored for incoming and outgoing calls. *If he has anything to hide, he will try to make sure it's still hidden.* Dunn thought to himself. He busied himself with reports and finishing up other cases while he waited for information on Henry.

"Dunn, a call came in from the hospital. Stacy wants to talk to you." Dunn looked up to see Helen, the station dispatcher, standing by his desk.

"Thanks, Helen." He got up quickly, put on his coat, and headed for the door. Jensen was still on vacation in Vegas with James; he would have to talk to Stacy alone.

When he arrived at the hospital, Dunn was shown to a private room with a large table in the middle. Dunn looked up into the corner of the room and saw the camera with the red light on, indicating it was recording. He got out his notepad and a pen while waiting for them to escort Stacy into the room. When the orderlies brought her in, Dunn noticed right away that she looked better, sober, and in a clear state of mind.

"Hello, Stacy. I'm glad you called. You look well." Dunn said as she sat down.

"Thanks." Stacy took her seat and waited for the orderlies to exit the room.

"I called you because I am feeling more myself now than I have in years and because my therapy is unlocking doors in my mind that I closed because I didn't want to face the truth behind them. I need to tell you what happened to Verona and my parents."

Dunn shifted in his chair. It was all going to come together. He picked up his pen and put it to the paper, eagerly waiting to hear Stacy's tale. She took a deep breath.

"For you to know the reasons why I first have to tell you about my childhood. My father was abusive, and this kick-started a lot of my mental issues. I struggled with bulimia and poor self-image; I purposely neglected my hygiene in hopes that he would lose interest. He never did. At sixteen, I moved out, began doing drugs to numb the pain, to forget, and maybe just to rebel. My mother saw a lot of this abuse-the physical and mental stuff- and she did nothing. She never spoke up against him or stood up for me.

When my drug addiction got so bad that I had nowhere to stay and nowhere else to turn, I went to the cabin. My parents never stayed there. They had their house in town, so I had the place to myself. Then, senior year, I dropped out. I did a lot of drugs and overdosed. Even though they weren't staying at the cabin, my parents came to check on me frequently. I think they just didn't want to be charged with abandonment or child endangerment.

They found me lying on the floor in a pool of my own vomit. They rushed me to the hospital, and since I was still seventeen, they signed me into the mental hospital. They told me it was for my own good and that I would be out when I got clean. I was in the hospital for over a year. I began hearing voices, seeing things, and couldn't tell what was real.

With medication and therapy, Dr. Hudson was able to control my symptoms, and I was finally released, but a condition of that release was that I had a place to live, so I went back to the cabin. My dad would stop by every day, sometimes to make sure I had food. Sometimes for other things. On one of *those* particular visits, I decided that I'd had enough. I made him a drink and laced it with crushed melatonin. I told him that the water heater wasn't working and asked him to look at it while he was there. He went to the basement, and I locked him in. He screamed and banged on the door, but he finally fell asleep because of the sleep aid in his drink, and when he did, I took a few five-gallon buckets to the basement and mixed a gallon of bleach and a gallon of ammonia in each. I held my breath and worked quickly.

When I got back upstairs, I sealed the basement door with plastic and duct tape to keep the fumes down there. I dumped his car at the bottom of the lake, along with his cell phone. My mom came looking for him the next day. She noticed the plastic on the basement door and started peeling it all off. I knew she was going to find him anyway. I let her open the door, and then I shoved her hard. I am sure she broke her neck on the way down because she didn't move when she hit bottom. I got rid of the buckets, aired the place out, and then closed the basement door and never opened it again.

The stench began the next day. I left the cabin and went to the crack house over on the east side of town. I got some heroin and stayed blitzed out of my mind for weeks. When I finally went back to the cabin, the smell was gone. I had almost forgotten that my parents were rotting in the basement. At that point, I had been off my meds for a couple of weeks, and the voices were back. It was hard to focus or know what was real. I went back to Dr. Hudson. He gave me a new prescription, and I got better once again.

I went to Henry's to see him. I made up a story about coming to see Verona, so he invited me in. I started flirting with him. I kept coming back while his wife was away for her art, and that flirting turned into more. We had an affair for more than a year. I wanted to hurt Verona; I thought destroying her family would be a good start, but I never intended to develop feelings for him.

Verona walked in on us once, and she was mad; she screamed at her dad, then me. I begged her just to leave and never say a word, but then she took pictures and threatened to send them to her mom. Henry rushed her and grabbed her phone; she went after him, and he grabbed her by the throat out of instinct.

Verona was coming at him like a wild animal; Henry was just trying to keep her away. She grabbed the phone from his hand, but before she could open the pictures to send them, I grabbed Henry's Autographed Sammy Sosa baseball bat, and I hit her. I heard her head crack, and she fell. She wasn't moving. Henry was in shock. He didn't want anyone to know what we did and what I did, so he helped me clean up and take her to the woods. We buried her over the edge of a hill in the woods where no one could see us digging from the road. Then we took the bat and her cell phone to the fire pit and burned them, along with the rug from Henry's office. We cleaned his office with bleach and made sure there was no evidence to be found. Henry was sure they would suspect Adam; he never liked Adam, so he didn't even feel bad about making him take the fall." Stacy cleared her throat. "May I get a glass of water, please?" She asked.

Dunn stared at her in shock. He didn't know what to say or what to do. She admitted to the crime and admitted that Henry helped her.

"I'll get you some water. Be right back." Dunn said. He stepped into the hall and walked away from the door so that Stacy could not overhear as he pulled out his phone. Dunn called the department and asked for someone to go pick up Henry. He asked for a copy of the recording from the conversation and then bought a water bottle from the vending machine.

When he went back into the room, Stacy was writing on the legal pad. Dunn sat the bottle of water in front of her. "Take your time. Put down as much detail as possible." Dunn said as he sat down across from her. When all that was left was signing her name to her statement, Stacy put her pen down.

"Can I get some kind of deal for telling you about Henry's involvement?" Stacy asked.

"That would be up to the DA. Sign your statement, and I'll see what I can do. We can probably get you sent to a locked-down mental facility instead of prison, but I can't promise you'll get no time." Stacy could see that either Dunn had empathy for her, or he was an outstanding actor. Stacy signed her name and passed the pen and pad back to Dunn.

"Okay. I have to take you in. You can come willingly and avoid the cuffs." She nodded and stood up. Dunn picked up the disc on their way out, and Stacy signed herself out of the hospital.

# CHAPTER TWENTY-THREE

Sara returned from Vegas jet-lagged and hungover. The details surrounding her trip with James were fuzzy at best, but she remembered his proposal very clearly. The whole flight back, Sara and James slept. Eventually, they would need to talk about what happened in Vegas, but it could wait for now.

James drove Sara back to her car, which she had left parked at the station. When they pulled into the parking lot, they saw a crowd gathered near the front doors.

"I should see what's going on in there," Sara told him. "I'll call you later." Sara went around the building to the side entrance. She saw Dunn just inside the front doors, preparing to make a statement to the press.

"What's going on?" Sara asked.

"Henry is gone; he's fled the country. He has created quite a paper trail too. Henry withdrew a substantial amount of cash and bought two bus tickets and three plane tickets to different locations. My guess is that he is on one of the planes or none of them. He could have used the cash and bought a ticket to anywhere in the world." Dunn sounded tired and frustrated as he spoke, and it was evident to Sara that he dreaded talking to the press.

"Have you already put out the BOLO? Let's get his photo plastered all over every news media outlet and in every airport and bus station around the world. Call the FBI, and let's get him added to the most wanted list." Sara suggested.

"I don't want to involve the FBI. Not if I don't *have* to," Dunn let out a deep breath and shrugged. "Here goes." He said as he walked out the front door into the barrage of questions and camera flashes.

Sara began looking through the file on Dunn's desk that contained his list of flights and bus tickets purchased with Henry's card. She found a photo of Henry online, printed it, and then faxed it to each of the airlines. She called each one to check the name on the ticket and see if someone had used it. The name on each ticket was different, and none of them was Henry. Jensen instructed them to flag each ticket and detain whoever was in the corresponding seat. She did the same thing with the bus tickets. Dunn returned from talking to the press and saw Sara working. From the look he gave her, she knew he was going to let her have it.

"What are you doing, Jensen?" He asked.

"Anyone who has used these tickets will be detained, and we can talk to them tomorrow," Jensen told him.

"Thank you, now go home. Your vacation isn't over until tomorrow." He pointed to the door.

"Okay, I'm going." Jensen smiled at him. "I'll be ready to go and talk to these guys tomorrow; hopefully, one of them will be Henry traveling under a false name."

"If we're lucky," Dunn said as Jensen headed for the door. "If we're lucky."

# CHAPTER TWENTY-FOUR

The lake was completely frozen, and the city had cleared the snow off of it and smoothed it for ice skating. Grant had only been ice skating a few times when he was a kid, but when Iris asked him to go with her to the Winter Wonderland night skate, he couldn't tell her no. Iris amazed him more every day. She didn't try to make him forget the pain he felt about Verona, but instead, she helped him through it. She was good to him, and he wanted to give her everything she wanted.

When they arrived at the lake, Grant spotted Adam and Riley too. Adam looked more apprehensive than Grant did. The girls went off together to rent skates from the portable rental shack.

"Hey Adam, how are you?" Grant clapped him on the shoulder.

"Good, you?" Adam responded. Grant could tell that he was lying, but they exchanged pleasantries all the same,

"You nervous about getting out there on the ice?" Grant gestured to the lake.

"No. It's just that..." Adam paused, "this is where..." Adam's voice trailed off again as he tried to shake out of it.

"Oh! I'm sorry, of course, Milan." Grant said.

"It's okay, let's just skate; I'm sure once we get out there, it will be better," Adam told him. They headed over to the rental shack. Iris and Riley were already tying their skates when Adam and Grant got in line.

"We'll meet you out there," Riley called as the two girls took off toward the ice.

Grant and Adam got their skates and laced up as quickly as they could. Adam watched Riley as she twirled effortlessly. He tried to focus on her, and only her, as he slid across the frozen lake to take her hand. Grant was not as suave. He slipped as he stepped onto the ice and then had to pull himself up on the barrier set up on the rink to outline it. Iris smiled and glided over to him.

"Need some help?" Iris reached out to Grant. He accepted, and hand in hand, they skated a whole lap around the rink until Grant found his balance.

"It's been a long time, but I don't remember ice skating being this hard." Grant laughed.

"That's because childhood makes you fearless," Iris said. Her hair was in loosely braided pigtails, and Grant loved how it framed both sides of her face. It made her look sweet and innocent but sophisticated. Grant moved closer to her and put his arm around her. He rested his hand on the small of her back as they drifted across the ice.

Music played from the loudspeakers on the rental shack, and when the owner bent down to plug in an extension cord, the trees, which he covered in white lights, lit up. It made the lake look like a winter wonderland. Riley and Iris both looked up at the artificial starry sky and smiled. Grant couldn't help but notice what a wonderful smile Iris had.

"I'm going to go get a hot cocoa; want one?" Adam asked, looking at Riley. She nodded and kissed him before he skated off to the other side of the ice.

"Would you like one? I will get it for you." Grant offered.

"I would love one, thank you." Iris smiled at him. Grant rushed over to get in line. By the time he reached the stand, Adam was already several people ahead of him in line. Grant could no longer see Iris and Riley through the crowd, so he focused on the task at hand. Adam ordered and had his drinks by the time Grant reached the counter.

"I'll see you back over there; I wouldn't want these to get cold." Adam raised his two cups of hot chocolate to Grant as he skated back across the lake. Grant just got his drinks in hand when he heard a crack, followed by several screams of panic. The crowd began to disperse quickly from the center, where Adam had not only spilled his cocoa but was now on his hands and knees with one skate in his hand. Adam was using the blade of his skate to crack the ice. His voice was desperate.

"Milan!" He screamed. "I'm here; I'll save you."

Grant began rushing toward him, but as he approached, he heard a loud and long crack as the ice splintered out from Adam and passed between Grant's legs. The damage stopped a few feet behind him. Grant tried to shift his weight, but the ice cracked again. He heard Iris and Riley both yelling from across the lake.

Iris had tried to rush out onto the ice, but Riley held her back, pointing out the danger. Adam now had a hole in the ice, roughly the size of a soda can. He plunged his hand down into the water, screaming for Milan to take his hand.

"Adam, Milan is gone." Grant tried to bring Adam back to reality.

"No, she's here; I heard her voice. She's screaming for help." He grabbed his skate again and began chipping away at the ice.

"Adam, Stop!" Grant yelled as the ice cracked loudly and split apart. Adam fell in as the ice parted, and in one lightning-quick moment, Grant found a sturdy place to step and dashed over to the hole. "Adam!" He called, plunging his hand down into the icy water. He felt around desperately for any part of Adam but felt nothing. He reached into his pocket and pulled out his phone, and turned on the flashlight. Grant laid it on the ice, illuminating the water. He saw Adam's shadow a few feet from the hole, and he seemed to be drifting further away.

Grant left his phone there on the ice and jumped into the water below. Grant swam to where Adam had drifted with adrenaline surging through his body and began dragging him back toward the light. The water was so cold it was stealing Grant's usual ability to hold his breath for a long time, and he began to panic as he felt the intense need to take a breath but was still too far from the surface.

He pushed through and finally got his face to the hole. He gasped for air and tried yelling for help, but breathlessness made it come out as more of a hushed whisper. Grant kept a hold on Adam's shirt as he pulled himself up from the hole in the ice. Then he bent down with two hands to hoist Adam out of the water. The crowd standing around the lake erupted in cheers, but Grant held up a hand for them to stop as he checked for a pulse. It was there, but it was weak.

Grant opened Adam's airway and gave him two breaths. Just as he pulled his mouth away, Adam coughed, spitting water everywhere. Adam sat up quickly, coughing out the rest of the water from his lungs, and grasped Grant's arm.

"You saved my life. I- I don't know what happened. I heard Milan calling for help; I saw her trapped beneath the ice. It felt so real. I know it wasn't, but at the moment, I couldn't tell." Adam looked in the direction of the crowd, scanning it for Riley. When he spotted her, Grant helped him to his feet on the side of the ice where it was still solid.

"Go, go talk to her," Grant said, giving Adam a nudge in her direction.

Adam skated over to where she stood as quickly as he could. Grant waited until they were off the ice and on their way to the rental shack to return their skates before he skated over to join Iris.

"Well, I'm sorry. I know this isn't exactly how you thought this evening would turn out." Grant smiled at her and shivered as the cold night air chilled him.

"This isn't exactly how I planned to get you out of your clothes, but whatever works, right?." Iris gave him a mischievous smile as she led him to the rental shack. Once they both had their shoes and said goodbye to Adam and Riley, Grant and Iris got into his car, and Grant turned the heat way up.

"Do you mind if I go home first to change out of these wet clothes?" Grant asked. "Maybe we could even watch a movie at my place, that is, if you are interested in continuing the evening?"

"I thought you'd never ask!" Iris teased as she slipped her hand into Grant's and interlaced her fingers with his. They drove back to Grant's house in a comfortable quiet; neither felt the need to fill the silence with small talk. Grant couldn't believe he had been so lucky to meet Iris. After what happened with Verona, he wasn't sure he would ever feel safe with another person.

Iris gasped as Grant pulled into his driveway and the head-lights passed over the grassy pasture where one horse stood. Iris stared at him happily as they drove down the driveway toward the house.

"Would you like to go for a ride?" Grant asked. "You could stay the night, and we could ride in the morning. That horse's name is Kodiak; he is most comfortable being by himself or in the company of humans. We tried to put him in a stall at night, but he freaks out. He has a lean-to over there where he will go for shelter when he wants to." Grant pointed to the large wooden structure attached to the side of the barn. There were support beams but no walls, and the roof was angled to keep snow from accumulating.

"How many horses do you have?" Iris asked.

"I have five. Kodiak, Juneau, Hope, Palmer, and Alyeska. They're all named after places I have been in Alaska." Grant explained as he stopped the car.

"Do you go to Alaska often?" Iris asked.

"I used to. The last time I went was just before Verona died. She had gone with me."

"I can imagine that the memories there would be difficult to think about still. I'm sorry you had to go through that; I can't imagine what it's like to lose someone you care for so deeply." Iris said.

Grant looked at Iris. She empathized with him, but behind that, he could see a hint of pain in her eyes. He touched her cheek and looked into her eyes. "I don't want to focus on the past. I want to focus on you." He leaned in and softly kissed her lips. She melted into him, satisfied with his response.

"Let's head inside; I'm freezing." Grant got out of the car quickly and rounded the vehicle to Iris's door. She smiled as he opened it for her.

"So chivalrous." She said.

"I try."

Grant led Iris into the den where he had his home theater set up. One wall had built-in shelves, and Grant had hundreds of DVDs. "Pick out anything you'd like to watch. Would you like something to sleep in, Iris? I am sure I could find you a t-shirt and maybe a pair of shorts." Iris smiled and nodded.

Grant returned in warm, dry pajamas. He handed a pair of fleece pajama pants and a t-shirt to Iris. "These might be a little big on you, but you can tie the strings," Grant said.

"Thank you." Iris kissed him on the cheek as she went to the bathroom that Grant pointed out to her. When she returned wearing Grant's pajamas, she saw that he had lit candles and grabbed a blanket and pillows for them to snuggle under on the couch.

Iris chose a movie, and Grant started it. They snuggled up on the couch together, and the heat from Iris's body warmed him. His touch sent shivers down her body, and she pressed against him. He stifled a groan as she guided his hands all over her body. She turned her face to his and pulled him into a deep kiss. Neither of them was even interested in the movie anymore as they explored each other. As soon as their clothes ended up on the floor, Grant's phone rang. He made no move to pick it up or look at it.

"Voicemail will get it. Don't worry about it." He reassured Iris that she had his full attention, but as soon as his phone stopped ringing, it started again. Grant let out a heavy sigh. "I'm sorry, it's late, and it must be important if they're calling back. Grant picked up his phone and looked at the caller ID. He saw Verona's picture and name on his screen, and in his shock and confusion, he almost dropped his phone.

"Hello?" Grant heard only heavy breathing on the other end of the line. "This isn't funny; who is this?" Again, there was nothing but the sound of breathing. Grant hung up and looked at Iris. She could see how terrified Grant was, and she felt the same way.

"What's wrong?" She sat up on the couch, clutching the blanket to her chest. "Who was it?"

"I don't know." He said. *Whoever it was, had Verona's phone, and the police might be able to track it.* Grant set his phone back down on the table beside the couch and sat down beside Iris. He took her in his arms, fully aware that the phone call had ruined the moment; he just held her and soon she seemed to have forgotten the call, but Grant thought about it all night.

# CHAPTER TWENTY-FIVE

Dunn received word from Grant first thing in the morning. Grant explained the phone call he had received from Verona and asked if they could take his phone and track the number. Dunn said they would do everything they could. Grant left his phone in the mailbox at the end of his driveway for them to pick up.

When Jensen arrived for work, she and Dunn drove out to Grant's house to pick it up. They saw Grant and Iris in the pasture riding horses. Grant waved to them as they grabbed the phone from the mailbox. Dunn waved in return, and then he and Jensen drove back to the station. Dunn sent the phone to their best technology specialist for analysis. He suspected that perhaps Henry had Verona's phone, and that's who called Grant, but he couldn't be sure until he got a location on the call.

Jensen and had interviewed the people who used the tickets purchased with Henry's card. They told her that someone -they wouldn't say who- paid them to use them and not to say more than that without a lawyer.

Henry had certainly done his homework in setting up this elaborate plan, and because of this, they were still no closer to him than the day he left; truthfully, they were likely farther away. Every day that passed made Dunn feel like they might never catch him. Jensen, as always, remained optimistic that they would find him. She was sure that he would mess up and give away some detail without meaning to.

Mrs. Warren was mourning. She had lost all three of her children and now her husband. She was alone. Madeline Warren cleared her schedule and sent all of her household staff home to their families. Other than the police, Madeline was not accepting visitors. Madeline liked Jensen's pleasant manner and spoke with her directly when Dunn and Jensen showed up to search the house. They had a warrant, although they didn't need it. Madeline was more than cooperative and wanted answers as much as everyone else.

"I can't believe that Henry would harm his own child to cover an affair," Madeline said to Jensen. "For years, he was the perfect husband, and I, myself, am not without shame. I, too, had an affair many years ago. It was right after Henry and I married, my parents had arranged our marriage from the time we were young to merge their companies.

Our parents always hoped that we would take over their businesses one day, but Henry wanted to write, and I am an artist. My parents and Henry's parents both run advertising companies. Henry worked in PR for a while, and then he began writing ads, jingles, and skits for different products.

That wasn't the kind of writing Henry wanted to do. He always said it sucked out his creative soul to sell other people's crap for them. Anyway, right after we got married, I was at an art show in Rome; I was swept away by this Italian artist named Domenico Romano. He thought I was a brilliant artist, and he invited me to a party with a lot of other big-name artists and a lot of lesser-known hopefuls too. He paraded me around on his arm, introducing me to everyone, including my favorite Urban 3D artist, Vesod. Dom and I spent a lot of time together that weekend, and our feelings for each other developed into something more than art appreciation.

When it was time for me to return home, the goodbye was bittersweet, and I wouldn't know for a couple of weeks, but I was pregnant. I confessed my transgression to Henry and that the child was possibly not his. He told me that no matter what, he would be the father. He didn't want to face the ruin a scandal might bring. I was thankful, but I couldn't stop thinking about Dom. I named Roman after his father's surname since his last name would be Warren.

Roman never knew that Henry wasn't his father. I gave the girls Italian names too so that Roman's name and parentage would never come into question. Henry loved his children, and he was a good father for many years; until the stresses of life hardened his heart. He became cold and distant from not just me but the children too. Luckily, they were grown then and needed us less, so it didn't affect them as it did me.

I resumed my travels and spent more time in Italy. Domenico had moved on; he married and had children. I saw him at a gallery opening in Florence, showcasing his latest sculptures. When our eyes met, he looked cornered. His wife and children were there, and it was obvious he did not expect, nor did he want the past to come back to haunt him. I never told him about Roman either, although I tried to write to him many times. I always ended up burning the letters, knowing what drama it would bring into our lives." Madeline wiped her eyes with a silk handkerchief.

"Sorry, dear, listen to me rambling on about the past. Would you please join me for tea in the kitchen?" Madeline asked. Jensen accepted eagerly, and they walked to the kitchen.

Madeline's kitchen was the most fantastic kitchen Jensen had ever seen. All of the appliances were top-of-the-line stainless steel, and the countertops were black marble. A large island dominated the center of the room and had bar stools on the three sides that did not face the cooking area. Madeline moved to the stove and put a kettle on.

"Mrs. Warren, how long has it been since you have had someone to talk to?" Jensen asked with genuine concern.

"Does my journal count?" She joked. "Please, you can call me Madeline."

"Do you have any real friends? Not just acquaintances, but people that you confide in?"

"I'm sorry, I am afraid the path of success in the art industry is a lonely one. I have been so busy traveling and meeting new people that I haven't had the time to bond with anyone enough to call them a friend."

"I think now, more than ever, it will be important for you to talk to someone. I can't imagine what this loss is like, but you shouldn't have to go through it alone. Perhaps we could look into some support groups, or maybe you could even talk to Dr. Hudson. He loved Milan, and if anyone knows a little of what you're going through, he would." Jensen suggested.

"It's kind of you to worry, but I have a better idea, you see, I trust very few people, so talking to someone new about these problems doesn't sound like something I would like to do. I find you to be a great listener, and for some reason, even though I don't know you very well, I feel like I can tell you anything. How about I call you once a week to talk? It will be my very first attempt at making a friend." Madeline smiled.

"That sounds nice," Jensen said. While Jensen and Madeline talked, Dunn and a few other officers went through everything in Henry's office. They collected his desktop computer, and the contents of his filing cabinet opened every book on the shelf, and used the black light and luminol spray to find blood traces. From the samples they collected, it appeared that the crime happened as Stacy had described. They packed everything up and carried it from the house. Madeline watched them as they took her husband's things but did not protest.

When Dunn got back to the station, he began searching through a manila envelope that he found on his desk. Jensen noticed his jaw drop as he read one of the pages he pulled out.

"I know where he is," Dunn said.

"From the look on your face, I would say it isn't good news," Jensen replied.

"Six Years ago, Henry opened a bank account in Brazil. One year ago, he applied for citizenship from naturalization. It was approved two weeks ago. He's untouchable now. They won't extradite him." Dunn slammed the papers on his desk and flopped down in his chair with a heavy sigh.

"Now what?" Jensen asked.

"I have no idea," Dunn told her.

"Maybe we can help." Dunn looked up from his desk to see Charlotte and Kristofer standing before him. Dunn got up and hugged Charlotte.

"I am so glad to see you two. This case has become a shit show." Dunn told them.

"So I heard. You have no jurisdiction in Brazil, and they won't extradite. Did I hear that correctly?" Charlotte asked. Dunn nodded. "I could go to Brazil, call it a bounty. You'll get your suspect, and I can add bounty hunter to my list of accomplishments. It's a win-win." Charlotte explained.

"Sounds like a start, but what's the plan? How will you find him, and how will you get him back? It's not like you can say pretty please and expect him to come willingly." Dunn said.

"You leave that to us. All we need are plane tickets and some spending money. We will just be tourists. Henry wouldn't recognize us, I am sure."

"I'll see what we can do. This plan just might work." Dunn said.

It took a few phone calls, but the treasurer approved the budget amount to capture the fugitive and wired it to the department within a day. Dunn purchased four plane tickets to Brazil on his credit card. He put half of their spending money on prepaid Visas, and the remaining cash was split four ways and then converted to Brazilian real.

"Let's meet at the airport. I will have your tickets; we can print them at check-in." Dunn said. They all agreed.

# CHAPTER TWENTY-SIX

Sara went to James's to spend the evening with him. She wasn't sure when she would be back, and they still needed to talk about what happened in Vegas. James had dinner ready when she got there, and the smell that greeted her when she opened the door was heavenly.

"What smells so delicious?" Sara asked, taking a long breath of it as she walked inside.

"I made a beef roast with carrots and potatoes, topped with onion, red wine, and fresh rosemary. James led her to the kitchen with excitement. He pulled the foil off the top of the roast, revealing the fruits of his labor.

"That looks amazing." Sara smiled at him as he pulled her to him and wrapped his arms around her. "I know you wanted to talk about what happened in Vegas, but let's enjoy dinner. We can talk after."

"I have something else I need to talk to you about, too," Sara said.

"Oh?" James looked nervous.

"The suspect in the case I am working on has fled the country. We have a private investigator working for us to capture and return him, but we can't let them go without protection. Dunn and I need to be there in case anything goes wrong." Sara explained.

"Mexico, or Canada?" James asked.

"Brazil. Because of their history of non-extradition."

"I see." James let his hands fall to his sides, and he looked like he felt rejected.

"What's wrong?" Sara tried to embrace him again, but he pulled away from her and started plating the roast.

"I expected a little anxiety about my proposal, or maybe even a rejection seeing how little we have talked since we got back, but this trip seems like convenient timing. I didn't expect avoidance." Sara began to object, but James sat Sara's plate down gently on the table. "Please, sit, let's enjoy dinner and save this talk for after. It seems we have a lot to discuss."

They ate in uncomfortable silence, each thinking about what to say to the other. Sara looked at James as he avoided her gaze. She watched the candlelight flicker across his face, and her heart ached. She ate what she could, but her stomach was in knots, and she ended up just pushing the food around on her plate. After dinner, James cleared their plates, put the leftovers away, and met Sara in the living room.

"I'm sorry," James said as he crossed the room and took her into his arms. "I'm just afraid." Admitting that was easier than he thought it would be. "I meant everything I said when I proposed to you, we might have been drunk, it might have been a spur-of-the-moment decision, but I don't take it back or regret a single moment." James tangled his fingers in Sara's long hair as he kissed her passionately. He lifted her into his arms and held her as she wrapped her legs around him. Sara pulled her lips back from his.

"I don't know what to say; I think I just need more time. I don't want to change how things are between us." She said, and she meant it. All the nerves melted away in his arms. James carried her to the couch and explored her body with his hands. Sara slid off of James's lap and laid down on the sofa, pulling him on top of her. She ran her fingers up under his shirt and caressed his back as he pressed against her.

"Do you have to go?" James groaned as his desire took over. He began undressing her, and she did not resist. She didn't want to think about leaving, not right now. James trailed kisses down her neck and across her collarbone, teasing her by touching her everywhere except where she wanted him to. Sara tucked her fingers into the front of his jeans and pulled his body against hers as she unbuttoned his pants and pulled them down past his hips. She reached for him, but he pulled away.

"Not yet. I want to make this night last." He grinned at her, and she moaned with desire as his words lit a fire inside her. It was hours before their hunger for each other was satisfied, and when it finally was, they lay together on a blanket on the floor of the living room.

"Sara, I know you have to leave for work, but I want you to know that I will be here missing you and thinking about you every second you're not here with me. I know that I want to be with you. I see us having a future, so I put in an offer on a house in the country today. It has five acres, an attached garage, a finished basement, four bedrooms, and two and a half bathrooms. That should be large enough for anything that comes our way." He touched her stomach, and she knew what he was implying.

"You want children?" She asked nervously.

"Only if that's what you want. I want you to be happy." James said. Sara knew that he meant it, she could tell, but she also saw the pain in his eyes and knew that the possibility of not having a family wasn't something he had considered.

"We have plenty of time for that," She said.

James drove Sara to the airport early the next evening. Neither of them had slept, but they also hadn't left the bedroom; there would be plenty of time for sleeping on the twelve-hour flight. Sara embraced James and kissed him deeply. "I'll miss you. And

I will call you when I can." She promised. James didn't want to let go of her, but he had to admire her professional drive. He nodded and backed away from her, blowing her a kiss before he turned to leave.

"So, How did it go last night? Are you engaged?" Dunn asked with a sly smile. Sara grinned and gave Dunn a weak backhand to his arm.

"No, I told him I needed more time." She smiled.

"I will admit, I was skeptical at first, but it seems like the real deal." He smiled at her.

Dunn handed Sara her ticket. "Our gate is 13B. We should head to it." Sara gathered her bags and went to the counter to check them. She kept out a blanket and a neck pillow. Dunn, Charlotte, and Kristofer did the same.

Once they were all seated, Sara made herself comfortable. She was exhausted. She was asleep before the wheels were even off the ground. Dunn used the quiet evening hours of the flight to do some reading on Rio de Janeiro. The first stop on their itinerary was the US Consulate there. Since they had no jurisdiction to apprehend Henry, their primary job was to protect Charlotte and Kristofer. Their contact at the consulate was more than happy to help. He was going to set them up with a surveillance van and equipment.

Henry's account was at the Bank of Brazil in Rio. They were unable to monitor activity on the account since Brazil had no obligation to divulge such information. Debit cards were easy enough to track if you knew how, but something told Dunn that Henry would need to use cash. There were some areas, like the favelas in the north, where it was dangerous to go. *If He's smart, Henry will go to the place where he is less likely to be found.* Dunn thought. He searched on his phone for remote areas near Rio. With a population of more than six million people, Rio already seemed an excellent place to hide. *It's going to be like looking for a needle in a haystack.* Dunn thought to himself.

Dunn finally gave in to sleep and was awakened by the sound of the meal cart coming down the aisle.

"Here's a copy of our in-flight menu. Would you like a drink or a snack?" The attendant asked.

Dunn took a coke and a pack of ginger cookies. He began looking over the menu.

"The ordering instructions are on the back of the menu; you can use the device here." The attendant gestured to the screen on the back of the seat in front of him. She smiled as she turned away and gave the same spiel to the passengers in the next row of seats. *Fancy.* Dunn thought as he began pushing buttons on the screen in front of him. He ordered a breakfast croissant sandwich and looked over at Jensen. "What did you order?" He asked.

"I got the crispy chicken bacon ranch wrap." She said. "So, what's the plan when we get there?" Jensen shifted her seat to the sitting position.

"From what I have read, Rio de Janeiro is a dangerous city to carry large sums of money. The bank is, by far, the best place to keep it. I have a contact at the consulate who will find out if Henry has a debit card for his Brazilian bank account. If he does, we will trace it, and then we will know every time he uses it. However, something tells me that he won't want us tracking him and will likely be using cash. The problem with cash is that it runs out eventually."

"And where will he have to go for more? The bank. So the plan is to stake out the bank while Charlotte and Kristofer visit the likely places an American might go in Rio?"

Dunn nodded. "I'm not sure it will work, but it's the best we have right now without the help of the Brazilian government. The US consulate holds little sway when it comes to protecting Brazilian nationals, and Henry is a Brazilian national now.

"Does Henry even speak Spanish?" Jensen asked.

"People in Brazil don't even speak Spanish; their official language is Portuguese," Dunn responded.

"Oh, wow. I didn't know that. I guess my Spanish phrasebook won't come in handy after all. I don't know any Portuguese, do you?" Dunn responded fluently in a foreign language that Jensen did not understand.

"How..." Before she could finish, Dunn interrupted.

"My wife was from Brazil. I learned for her. She married me for citizenship; I'm pretty sure. I loved her, though. She was beautiful and kind. Until she was certain her citizenship was permanent, then she left me for some young guy from California. It broke my heart. We sold the house and split the money, I had no need for a whole house for just me, and she wanted to move to California."

"I'm sorry to hear that. It sounds like you tried to make it work, even learned another language for her. That's sweet." Jensen said, trying to reassure him.

"I think I prefer to be on my own anyway. It's easier to pick up and go on trips like this when there's no one waiting for you at home." Dunn nudged her with his elbow, and Jensen knew he was referring to James.

"Yeah, he was a little hurt by the timing of the trip given his recent marriage proposal and the holiday season being so near, but I think we worked through it." She said, smiling as she thought about their night together. "He put an offer in on a house for us. A nice place in the country, quiet, and with quite a bit of land." Jensen said.

"So things *are* pretty serious then, so why didn't you guys just get married by Elvis in Vegas?" Dunn laughed.

"What?" Jensen pretended to be offended, but she couldn't keep a straight face, and she laughed too.

"Yeah, We haven't even met each other's families yet," Jensen said. "I think my mom would kill me if I got married to someone she has never met and then didn't even invite her to the wedding."

Dunn nodded. "That probably wouldn't go over well." Their conversation was interrupted by the arrival of their breakfast. Jensen was starving and began eating right away. Sara realized that the last time she had a meal, she had been so nervous about the looming conversation that she hadn't consumed more than a few bites. Jensen finished her wrap before Dunn was even halfway through his croissant.

Six hours into the flight, everyone began to get restless. Their layover was still an hour away, but Dunn couldn't stand it; he stood up in the aisle and stretched his legs. Jensen did the same. Other passengers began standing as well, and the conversations grew louder. The flight seemed to stretch on forever. They had an overnight layover in Panama; they would have eight hours to walk and eat before the other six-hour flight to Rio.

Sara sat back down and put her earbuds in her ears. She turned on her playlist and drifted back to sleep. When Sara woke this time, it was the bump of the landing gear on the pavement that roused her. She looked over at Dunn, who gathered his belongings, and she heard Kristofer and Charlotte shuffling in the seats behind them to do the same.

When they exited the plane, it was near dinner time. Dunn, Sara, Charlotte, and Kristofer walked around the airport, taking in the sights and smells. They weren't ready to sit again. Jensen noticed that most of the signs were in Spanish, but there were

English translations. She was thankful for that. Jensen looked in all the stores and found a few souvenirs to bring back with her.

"You should have bought those on the way back; what if you lose them?" Dunn asked.

"What if I spend all my money? Then I wouldn't have enough on the way back." She was half-joking, but only half. Dunn picked up a pair of aviator sunglasses.

"What do you think?" Dunn asked.

"You look like Farva from Super Troopers." She chuckled as he took the glasses off and put them back on the shelf.

"I can't unsee that now, thanks." He joked. Charlotte and Kristofer met them outside the shop.

"We rented a car; Since we have such a long layover, we saw no reason to stay at the airport. I made reservations at Nacion Sushi. We can get some dinner, go sightseeing, and then be back well before our connecting flight." Charlotte said.

"Sounds great! Thanks, Charlotte." Jensen said. Dunn groaned.

"Sushi? Not a fan." He said.

"They have steak and chicken too; you could always get stir fry," Jensen said.


The evening went by too quickly. It began with dinner, continued with drinks, and then, they drove around the beautifully lit city. The reflection on the water of the city lights made the ocean look like a sea of stars. "Someday, I have to come back here on an actual vacation," Jensen said.

"Maybe it can be a honeymoon." Dunn smiled.

"If we get married." Jensen reminded him, with emphasis on *if.*

"Wait, James proposed?" Charlotte asked in shock.

"He sure did! While they were in Vegas. They could have been married by Elvis!" Dunn exclaimed.

"That happened so quickly." Charlotte seemed worried. "You're not pregnant, are you?"

"What? No." Jensen was shocked by the question. "He's buying a house in the country. He's already thinking about having a family and living happily ever after. I just don't know If I'm ready for all that."

"Don't let him rush you; if it's right, you'll know, and there's plenty of time to get married and have kids; you're young!" Charlotte smiled. Kristofer turned in his seat to look at Jensen.

"I guess that means I still have time to sweep you off your feet." He said with a wink. Jensen laughed. Before too long, they were all back at their terminal, ready to board their next flight, nonstop to Rio.

# CHAPTER TWENTY-SEVEN

The plane touched down in Rio in the early evening. The drive from the airport to the consulate was another half hour. Dunn was cranky and tired, but he knew their hotel awaited them after the long flight as soon as this meeting at the consulate concluded. They would need at least a day to recover from the flight before they got to work.

The consulate building was a tall and narrow rectangle standing between two broader and more aesthetically pleasing structures. Dunn called the consulate when they arrived, and the representative instructed them to leave all electronics in the vehicle, including their cell phones. Two men wearing black suits, sunglasses, and earpieces showed them inside and to a small office on the fourth floor.

A woman entered the room, pushing a cart full of equipment that was all boxed up and ready to be loaded into the surveillance van.

"My name is Cathy Harmon; I am the assistant consul general. Welcome to Rio de Janeiro. I hope your travel here wasn't too taxing." She didn't wait for a response before continuing with the briefing.

"Other than offering you the equipment need to conduct your business here, the consulate can in no way involve ourselves in the apprehension of your suspect. Finding and apprehending him will be your responsibility alone. As I am sure you know, Brazil does not extradite its nationals, and your suspect's newly acquired citizenship makes your task more difficult, but not impossible. If you manage to apprehend your suspect, we have a US Marshall ready to escort him immediately back to the United States. Brazil doesn't want another murderer on the streets, I am sure, so as long as you arrest him without incident, we can get him back to the states."

Cathy's hair was blond and shoulder-length. She wore black, plastic-framed glasses and a black pantsuit. The only thing in her outfit that wasn't black was the string of pearls around her neck. She ordered two guards to load up the van and handed Dunn the keys.

"Good luck," Cathy said and turned from the room; her heels echoed clicks down the hall until she was gone from their auditory range.

Dunn drove the van to the hotel and parked in the back of the lot in a well-lit area. Sara was ready for some much-needed relaxation. She went with Charlotte to the spa, and they soaked in the hot tub, sat in the sauna, and even got a facial while the guys went to the hotel bar. Their rooms were next to each other, Charlotte and Sara in one and Dunn and Kristofer in the other. They enjoyed their last free evening; tomorrow, the work would begin.

Charlotte and Kristofer got up early the next morning, ready for their first day exploring. First on their list was Christ the Redeemer. There was little hope of finding Henry there, but Charlotte could not travel to Rio and not see it for herself. From there, they would take a taxi to the center of town, buy food from one of the street carts, or maybe multiple street carts, and then find a local to show them around. Their goal was to learn the city's layout and report back at the end of the day. *Not a bad day on the job.* Charlotte thought as she and Kristofer waited for their taxi.

Dunn and Jensen's job for the day was not so fun. They were on a stakeout of the bank where Henry had his account. They sat in the van most of the day, watching everyone who entered and left the bank. Dunn got a phone call from his contact at the consulate, not the woman they had met during their briefing, but Someone Dunn would not name.

"Henry has a debit card. He has been using it near Alemão in the Northern zone. He has been using the cable car to commute." Dunn said.

"Isn't that the most dangerous favela in Rio?" Jensen asked. Dunn nodded.

"It would be dangerous for us both of us to go in, and you have a look that just screams 'cop.' Maybe I could take a walk around the favela and ask some people. I will say I am looking for my father. Verona and I were about the same age."

"It's dangerous, but it could work. I would feel safer if you wore a wire." Dunn said. And maybe take Kristofer with you."

Jensen agreed. The consulate people warned them that the favelas were dangerous, lawless places where gangs and drug traffickers ruled the streets. They told them not to venture into them, especially in the north zone. Dunn and Jensen continued watching the bank until it closed, then they headed back to the hotel to meet up with Charlotte and Kristofer.

They laid the plans for tomorrow's search and then went to bed, but sleep evaded Sara for several hours. She tossed and turned, trying to rest, but her mind would not stop. She was terrified of what she had to do but knew it was their best chance to find Henry.

Dunn collected all the information he could about the favela while Kristofer slept. The local police have made several attempts to pacify the north zone, but none have been successful. The heavily armed officers' presence has seemingly brought more violence between the police and suspected drug traffickers; the government cycles between pacification and pulling police presence. No matter how many attempts they make, the area is still under the control of the Red Order's gang members. The gang takes care of the people in the favela, and in return, no one speaks out about their illegal activities. Dunn finally forced himself to sleep. *I can't keep Sara safe if I fall asleep on the job.* Dunn thought.

The next morning, Sara tried her best to dress like she belonged in Rio, like she was from the favela. She wore a black tank top, old denim shorts, and sneakers. Sara planned on doing a lot of walking and wanted to be comfortable. Dunn taught her a few phrases in Portuguese, and they practiced until she could say them correctly.

"Have you seen this man?" Dunn asked Sara. She repeated in Portuguese.

"Você viu esse homem?"

"Good," Dunn said. "Now say; he is my father."

"Ele é meu pai," Sara repeated.

"If you ask this one first, you won't need the other two if the answer is yes. Do you speak English?"

"Você fala inglês."

"Great job. I guess you're ready." Dunn said. He handed her a small recording device that was no bigger than a button. It has a small wire as long as a bread tie.

Sara went to the lobby restroom and placed the wire in the band of her bra. She made sure it wasn't visible and then said, "Testing" Sara's text tone chimed. Dunn was letting her know that they could hear her. She walked back to the van. As she got close to where they were parked, a high-pitched squeal emitted in Dunn's headphones, and he quickly turned the equipment off.

Sara and Kristofer took a taxi into the north zone. The main streets of the favela were clean and seemed peaceful. When they got to Complexo do Alemão, they got out of the taxi and continued on foot. Dunn had followed in the van, keeping a fair distance; he parked the van on the main street and turned on the surveillance equipment. Dunn could hear the voices of the people around Sara and Kristofer and their footsteps on the pavement. Dunn had no idea what range the small audio device had, but they were about to find out.

Sara and Kristofer began walking up the main street, taking in the sights that were so different from the city, a kind of organized chaos. Wires, bunched together in knots, spanned across the buildings' tops, and houses were built on top of other houses, towering shanties up the mountainside. The sides of the buildings and even the streets in some places had large murals painted on them. Sara and Kristofer turned off the main street into a narrow alleyway, and almost instantly, the view changed. The alley was unpaved, a dirt road littered with garbage alongside the buildings. Crooked cement staircases came from every direction, leading up to each level of shanties. Doorways half-hidden by stairs caused people to duck their heads as they entered or exited. Sara and Kristofer climbed the narrow stairs that continued up the alley, and as it twisted around to the right, they heard the sounds of people and music. The passage ended, and Sara and Kristofer stepped out onto another paved street. A strong and wonderful aroma wafted to them and made them hungry. Restaurants and shops lined the road, and people talked happily. The music came from a small building with no doors or windows, just open passages where windows and doors would usually be. A man was teaching a group of kids to dance in a Latin-infused hip-hop style. Sara stopped outside the doorway to watch. She saw the happiness on the children's faces and the instructor's patience, and it warmed her heart. The children saw her watching, and a couple of them waved. The instructor came over to her, speaking Portuguese, and took her by the hand, pulling her into the studio.

"Você fala inglês?" She asked, hoping that her pronunciation was correct and that he understood.

"Yes. I do. Dance with me, please. "He put his hand on her waist, grabbing her other hand in his. He led her in an impromptu dance step, which she was surprisingly able to follow. He twirled her and released her from his grasp, and applauded. When he clapped, the kids did too, and they smiled at her.

"Thank you for that demonstration; you are a lovely dancer." His accent made her weak at the knees, and she smiled at him.

She waved and backed out of the classroom so they could continue their lesson.

Sara pulled the photo of Henry out of her pocket. As they walked up the street, she began showing the picture to everyone. "Você viu esse homem? Ele é meu pai." They all glanced at the photo for less than a second before shaking their heads or telling her no. Sara kept trying; she did the same thing on the next paved street with no luck. As they walked up the row of shops, a convoy turned down the road. The cars all had tinted windows. The back windows of each vehicle were halfway down, and assault rifles rested on the windows. No one panicked. The people here acted as if this were an everyday occurrence, but Sara froze with fear as Kristofer moved between her and the street.

When the cars disappeared without incident, Sara continued her search. She noticed police officers, also armed with assault rifles, and went to ask them. She showed them the picture and asked the questions Dunn had taught her to ask. They did not speak English, but they began to tell her something in Portuguese. Sara held up a finger and ran back to the dance studio with Kristofer chasing after her. The instructor had just dismissed the class and was gathering his belongings when she approached.

"I didn't expect to see you again so soon. Couldn't resist, could you?" He smiled and did a salsa step toward her; beads of sweat made his skin glisten, highlighting his muscle tone. He was not wearing a shirt now, and Sara could feel her heartbeat quicken, and she watched his hips sway as he approached. Kristofer remained outside but kept his eyes fixed on Sara.

"I need your help. I can pay you." She pulled out a few notes that she had in her pocket. She had no idea how much it was, but his eyes widened at the sight of it. He took it from her hand and shoved it into his pocket.

"How can I help?"

"I need a translator. I have not been able to find too many English-speaking locals, including the police. I am looking for my father." Sara showed him the picture. "Have you seen him?"

"No, sorry. I will gladly translate for you, but I do not talk to the police." *If he only knew.* Sara thought. "My name is Sara; what's yours?"

"Angelo. Who's your friend?" He asked, gesturing to Kristofer.

"This is Kristofer; he is helping me find my father." She told him.

"Lead the way, Sara."

"I need to know what the policeman was saying to me. He was trying to tell me something, but I didn't understand. If you could please just listen and tell me what he said, you will not have to talk to him, I promise." Sara said. Angelo sighed, nodded his head, and followed Sara back out where Kristofer was waiting.

They went back to the officer, and she asked again. The officer repeated what he said before. Angelo turned Sara to face him. "He said; a man could hide forever in the favelas because they are so large and contain so many people. He said, good luck," As Angelo translated, the convoy they saw earlier passed by again. This time, they noticed the police officers and fired their weapons into the crowd. Screams erupted from the shops as people began to scatter. Angelo grabbed Sara as the shots deafened her. Angelo tried to pull her off of the street and into a nearby shop. She turned back to grab Kristofer's hand and pull him away too, but he crumpled to the ground. Blood started spilling onto the pavement from his abdomen.

"Kristofer! No!" Sara screamed and tried to go to him, but Angelo held her back.

"Not yet; it might not be over." He was right. More gunshots followed as the police opened fire on the lead car. The driver revved his engine and plowed into the officer firing at him. There was a sickening crunch as his legs broke under the hood of the car. Sara screamed and buried her face into Angelo's chest. He led her back behind the counter. They ducked down behind it, and he held her until all was quiet. When the gunfire stopped and the cars were gone from the street, Sara and Angelo made their way back outside. Kristofer lay there in the street, his blood pooling around him. Sara ran to him; she dropped to her knees beside him and felt for a pulse. There was no sign of life left in him.

Angelo helped Sara to her feet. "I'm sorry about your friend. Let's get him out of here."

Angelo picked up Kristofer like he was a bag of corn and put him over his shoulder, and began walking back toward the city.

"What the hell was that?" Sara demanded, gesturing behind them as they walked.

"Recently, the Brazilian government has been trying to *pacify* the favelas. They bring in militarized police units, make tons of arrests, and many are killed as they try to take back territory from the gang that controls the favela." Angelo explained. "When the police leave us alone, it's mostly peaceful, unless another gang tries to overstep their boundary. The government usually forgets about us, and even though it would be nice to have all of the advantages the people of the pavement have, we have a community here. We help each other and care for each other. Even the gang members take care of people here.

They aren't as horrible as people think; they're more like a militia fighting against social injustice. The money to help people has to come from somewhere, though, and there are no jobs in town for people like us. The city people turn their noses up at us and look down on us like we are less than the dirt beneath their designer shoes. They even built walls around the border of the favelas in some areas to separate from us so they can pretend we don't exist."

"I'm sorry to hear that. That sound's awful. As much as you say, the gang members help the community; they also hurt it. Drugs destroy lives and enslave people to dependency. Why would they want that?" Sara asked.

"Money, control. If they don't have what people want, people will go elsewhere to get it. That leaves an opening for another gang to seize control; a gang that doesn't care what happens to us or our businesses." He said.

When they got to the edge of the city, Angelo put Kristofer down with care. "You can call an ambulance and have them meet you here. I have to get back. I'm sorry again, I will ask around about your father. Can I have your number? You know, in case I come up with anything." Angelo asked. Sara put her hand out for Angelo's phone and put her number into it. Angelo thanked her, smiled, and then disappeared back into the alleyways of the favela.

"Okay, Dunn, My GPS on my phone is active; I'm sending my location for immediate extraction." She whispered toward the wire she still wore in her bra. Sara dreaded seeing Charlotte as the van pulled up beside her, and as expected, Charlotte was distraught. She sobbed at the sight of Kristofer as Dunn and Sara loaded him into the back of the van. She rushed back to his side, laying her hand on the side of his face; she cried as Sara had never heard anyone cry in her life. The ride to the hospital was the longest ride of her life, and the air was heavy with grief.

They rushed inside, and Dunn told them what happened. They brought out a gurney, and Dunn opened the back of the van for them. As they placed Kristofer on the gurney, they covered him with a white sheet.

His body was sent directly to the morgue. The bullet had gone straight through; there was an entry and an exit wound. The mortician stitched the holes and started the process of preparing the body for burial. Kristofer was an organ donor, and there happened to be a long list of people here in Brazil who needed organs. The doctor discussed this with Charlotte.

"Ma'am, the organs would not be viable by the time they got back to the states. I know you never intended to help a person outside your own country, but if you agree, I promise we will match them to someone who needs them desperately." The doctor told Charlotte.

"His organs should be used. If they wouldn't make it back home, at least I will know that a part of my brother lives on." Charlotte said. The doctor thanked her and offered her a gentle hand on her shoulder before walking away.

Charlotte had her brother cremated; the ashes came in a heavy black box with a sealed lid. They did not work for the next few days. Charlotte held a wake for her brother at a bar in the city. Three were in attendance. They drank, and Charlotte talked about all of the good times they had together. She even told stories about how they didn't always get along. Charlotte was quite a bit older than Kristofer, so they didn't spend a lot of time together as children. The two of them became close in adulthood. They laughed, they cried, and then they drank some more. On day three of their grief bender, Angelo called Sara. She left her seat at the bar in search of a quieter corner.

"How are you holding up?" He asked.

"Okay, I guess. Did you find anything?"

"Yeah, some of the guys heard a man asking around for a priest. He fit your description. He was very adamant that it had to be a catholic priest and that he didn't want to go into town and draw attention to himself. Does that sound like your guy?"

"I'm not sure. Any Idea where those people sent him?"

"Well, there is only one catholic church around here. We could ask. I promise to keep you safe." Angelo said.

Sara knew it was a risk going back into the favela, which Dunn and Charlotte would be apprehensive about taking. Sara looked over at her friend and partner. They were drunk, laughing together, and didn't even realize that she had stepped away to take a call. Sarah pulled the blood-stained photo of Henry out of her clutch and looked at it.

"Meet me at the border in fifteen minutes."

# CHAPTER TWENTY-EIGHT

Angelo was waiting at the border of the favela when Sara's taxi arrived. The favela looked different at night but still very much awake. Sara noticed men openly dealing drugs and selling guns with AK47s strapped to them. Angelo saw her apprehension.

"You're safe. You're with me." He put an arm around her shoulders and led her past the drug dealers; they slipped up the alley behind them. The dealers nodded to Angelo as they passed. Sara was suddenly uncomfortable, she felt like maybe she had just walked into a trap, but she didn't voice her concerns. She was put a little at ease when the catholic church became visible.

Angelo and Sara walked up to the front doors, and to Sara's surprise, they opened. She looked over at Angelo with obvious shock on her face.

"God never sleeps, and you never know when someone might need him." Angelo smiled, and any apprehension she felt when she was walking up the dark alley with him melted away. A priest stepped out of the background as the bell over the front doors rang. He said something in Portuguese.

"He says, Welcome children of God. Have you come for confession?" Angelo translated.

He spoke back in Portuguese, and the priest nodded. "Show him the photo of your father," Angelo told Sara. She pulled the photo out, and the priest took it and held it in his hands. The priest looked nervous, and as he spoke, Angelo translated for Sara.

"He is not here. He was, but I couldn't help him. I told him I would have to send for another priest, and it could be weeks before one arrived with experience enough to do what he was asking."

"Ask him what my father was looking for, what did he need?"

"He was looking for an exorcist." Angelo's eyes grew wide with shock.

"Where did he go?" Angelo repeated Sara's question to the priest.

"He said he was renting the space above the shop a few blocks down."

"Which shop?"

"The grocery, Mimosa's, come on, let's go," Angelo said. He led Sara to the large double doors. The drug dealers they passed on the street earlier met them on the stairs, pointing their weapons at Sara and Angelo. They spoke to Angelo, and Sara understood only one word. Policia. Angelo looked at Sara with hurt in his eyes. "Is it true? You're a cop?"

"Yes, but in America, not here. I have no jurisdiction here; I'm just looking for my father. How did they know?" Sara asked.

"They saw you get into the van with that other cop the day your friend was killed. They have eyes everywhere; when I said I don't talk to cops, I meant it. No one here talks to cops." He had barely finished his sentence when one of the gang members walked up behind him and knocked him out with a well-aimed buttstroke from his gun.

Sara screamed as they closed in on her. The priest yelled from the back of the cathedral, and one of the gang aimed their gun at him. He put his hands up and backed away. "I will pray for you, my child," Sara heard him say before the painful thud that made everything go black.

Dunn and Charlotte realized soon enough that Sara had left. They returned to the hotel looking for her but found no evidence that she had been there. He dialed her number. It went straight to voicemail. He logged into the locate device feature on his phone and typed in her information. "Her last location before the signal was lost was this church," Dunn said, showing Charlotte the ping on his digital map. "We have to go find her." Dunn noticed that, while the application had labeled the church's location, there were no directions to it available. Charlotte held her head in her hands in frustration.

"What would make her take off like that without telling anyone?" Charlotte complained.

"I don't know, but I have a bad feeling." Dunn grabbed his gun, hid it in the waistband of his shorts, and headed for the van. Charlotte reluctantly followed. Dunn had already started the van when Charlotte got to it, and she barely had time to buckle before Dunn was pulling out of the parking lot. She glanced in the back where her brother's blood still stained the floor, and she felt the anxiety build up in her.

Dunn parked the van in the same spot they had picked up Kristofer. They walked up the same street that Angelo had led Sara. Dunn looked at his GPS and took a right through an alleyway. When they reached the church, Charlotte opened the door for Dunn. The bell rang, and the priest appeared.

"How can I help you? Have you come for confession?" The priest asked in Portuguese.

"No, we are looking for the girl that was here a little while ago. Can you tell me where she went?"

"The Red Order."

"Where is that?"

"Not where, *who*." The priest answered.

"They are the gang that controls this area. The gang took the girl at gunpoint. I tried to stop them, but they threatened my life, and had I tried anything, they would have ended hers."

"I understand. Where can I find The Red Order?" Dunn asked.

"They are everywhere, and they see everything. Be careful." The priest warned.

"She was looking for a man. Do you know if she had any luck?"

"He's renting the space above the market. I told her that, but she didn't get to check it out."

"Thank you." Dunn turned and walked back toward the door.

"Is it really smart to go looking for the gang members who killed my brother? You heard the gunfire; they arm themselves with automatic rifles; there is no way we can take them with your six-shooter."

"It's not a six-shooter; it's a 9mm. I have at least fifteen rounds." Dunn said.

"You know what I mean." Charlotte objected.

"I know, but you know Sara, and you would have me leave her fate in the hands of the people who murdered Kristofer for standing near a cop? What if they find out Sara is a cop? She will be as good as dead. I have to find her." Dunn was relentless, and Charlotte could no longer argue. They walked back out of the church and down the alleyway. Charlotte grabbed his arm as a convoy of vehicles approached on the cross street. Guns were sticking out both sides, and the cars paraded down the road, establishing their presence.

"That's The Red Order. We can't take on all of them. We need backup. Maybe your contact at the consulate could help?" Charlotte pleaded, and Dunn could see that she was terrified. He let out a deep sigh.

*Wherever you are, Sara, stay strong. I promise I'm coming for you.* Dunn thought. They turned down the main street and walked quickly back to the van.

"We'll get them looking for Sara, and we can come back when it's light and look for Henry," Dunn said as he started the van and headed back to the hotel. He texted his contact at the consulate and sent him a picture of Sara.

# CHAPTER TWENTY-NINE

Sara woke to pitch black with her hands bound behind her back, and there was some kind of cloth over her head. She tried to loosen the ropes around her wrists to no avail. Sara tried to scream, but the gag in her mouth intercepted it, and her scream was nothing more than a muffled whine. She heard a shuffling behind her.

"Who's there?" She tried to ask, but her words came out as incomprehensible grunts. The grunts that answered in response told her that it was Angelo. She wiggled her body in his direction, moving back and forth like a snake through the sand. When she was able to touch him, she realized they were back to back. She reached for the ropes that bound his hands. She might not be able to untie her own, but maybe his bonds would be easier.

Sara began pulling at what she thought were the sides of the knot, but she couldn't see, which made the task nearly impossible. She thought she had just started to make progress when they heard footsteps coming in their direction. Sara and Angelo quickly started wiggling their bodies back to their positions. They lay there quietly as if they were still unconscious. Sara heard the man; he was on the phone. She couldn't understand the conversation, but she recognized that the man was calling the person on the other end of the phone by what she thought might be a name. Patrão. Sara said it over and over in her mind so that she would not forget. The man on the phone walked back out and slammed the door behind him.

Sara's arms felt hot, and there was the familiar tickle of blood dripping down her arms. Wiggling her body across the floor to reach Angelo had caused deep abrasions on her arms, but she had to try again; they didn't have much time. Angelo knew this much to be accurate, so he met her halfway, moving in the same way she had. Their hands met once more, and Sara quickly tried to untie Angelo's hands. She became frustrated and cried as her fingers fumbled. Finally, she found the right notch in the knot, and it came loose. Angelo quickly shook his bonds and began untying Sara.

Once her hands were free, she removed the black cloth covering her head and the gag that had been giving her cotton mouth for the last hour. Angelo helped her to her feet, and they both began searching the room for a way out. They were in a small storage room with a concrete floor. Shelves lined the walls around the room, but they were all empty. Above one of the racks, there was a vent in the ceiling. Sara pointed it out.

"Do you think we could get out that way?"

"Maybe, it's worth a shot." They rushed over and climbed the shelf. Angelo moved the arm that locked the vent closed, and it swung open, hinged on one side. He hoisted Sara up, and she crawled into the vent. Angelo pulled himself up after her and put his fingers through the bars of the grate to lock it back into place. Sara and Angelo crawled through the ducts slowly, trying not to make too much noise.

They heard voices and loud music from below them. It smelled like cigar smoke and spilled liquor. Light poured into the vent ahead, and Sara looked down into the room as she quietly passed. A large table dominated the middle of the room; it was covered with stacks of money and packages of drugs. *There must be over a million dollars worth of notes and drugs in there!* Sara thought.

Angelo tapped her leg and pointed to a fork ahead. He gestured to the right, where the vent system sloped upward. Sara turned right and crawled until the vent ended and the fresher air from outside swept away the stench of cigars. The vent opened onto the roof. As they crawled out of the small space, they heard a commotion from below. Trucks roared to life, and dogs began barking loudly.

"I think they realized we escaped," Sara said. Angelo Walked around the entire roof.

"The vent is the only way up here; there isn't even a fire escape. Come here." Angelo went to the middle of the roof and laid down. He patted the concrete beside him. Sara lay down beside him and looked up at the sky as the chaos below continued to spread in every direction.

"They will have people out looking for us all night. If we stay here, they will assume they lost us by morning, and hopefully, we can escape when the sun comes up."

"Won't it be easier for them to spot us during the day?" Sara asked.

"No, most of the gang activity happens at night; they sleep in until at least noon," Angelo said. The longer they lay still, the cooler the night air became. Sara moved in and put her head on Angelo's chest. Angelo wrapped her in his arms to keep her warm. She felt him kiss the top of her head gently.

"When that guy was on the phone, I heard him say a name, Patrão. Do you know who he is?"

"No, that just means 'boss' he was probably talking to the gang leader though."

Sara looked up at Angelo.

"What made you want to start teaching dance?" Sara asked.

"The biggest reason is that when kids have nothing to do, no outlet, they turn to drugs. The more kids I can keep busy and away from the gangs, the better for everyone."

"That's sweet. How many kids do you teach?"

"I have about twenty total between the two classes."

"What about you? Besides being a cop, is there anything you enjoy?" Angelo asked.

"I like reading. I'm pretty boring, I guess."

"Never." Angelo pulled her closer. Their mouths were only inches apart, and his arms felt so warm and safe. Angelo leaned in, and Sara wanted to kiss him. He was kind, brave, and an incredible dancer, and she found him irresistibly handsome. He pressed his lips to hers, and she kissed him back. An electrifying tingle swept over Sara's entire body, and she pulled him closer with urgency. His hand wandered up her shirt and found her breast, and suddenly, Sara thought of James and pulled away.

"I'm sorry; it was just the adrenaline of making it out of there alive, knowing they're looking for us and being right above them the whole time. I just got swept up. Again, I apologize, I don't remember you saying it, but I'm pretty sure a gorgeous girl like you already has a boyfriend. I over-stepped." Angelo rambled.

Sara wanted to give in and kiss him again just to shut him up. Still, she thought about James waiting for her at home, having Thanksgiving dinner without her as the weather got cold and snowy, and here she was, in Brazil, wearing shorts and a tank top, laying on a rooftop under the stars with Angelo.

"I do have a boyfriend; he proposed, actually." She told Angelo.

"I knew it." Angelo smiled at her and put a little distance between their faces, but he still kept her wrapped in his arms. At some point during the night, it became quiet enough to sleep. The sun came up, and the heat of the early morning sun roused Sara from her slumber. She stretched and sat up, looking over at Angelo, who was also just waking up.

"I guess we should get going," Sara said. Angelo nodded and stood up. He went over to the edge of the building, then motioned for Sara to join him.

"There's a truck down here, and we can jump down on top of it, then climb down. It will probably make some noise, so we will have to be quick." Angelo reached out for Sara's hand. "I'll go first so I can catch you." Angelo jumped down onto the roof of the truck, and his feet thumped as they connected with the metal. Angelo reached up for Sara. "Come on; I got you." Sara jumped off the roof and into Angelo's arms. When she stood up, their faces were so close together; she could feel his breath on her lips. She quickly turned away, ending the moment and refocusing her attention on their daring escape.

They climbed down from the truck and started running. "If we can make it to the alleyways, we can get all the way down to the city without using the main streets. We will want to avoid those." Angelo led the way from the warehouse near the top of Alemao through the winding alleys and staircases beside the shanty houses.

"We will have to cross the main street here, but I don't see many people out and about yet, so we may have time as an advantage," Angelo told her. "We are going to walk out together, act natural, and don't draw attention." Angelo took Sara by the hand and led her across the street to the adjacent alley where their descent continued.

Gunfire erupted behind them; a few bullets lodged into the shanty houses just above their heads. The gunfire was followed by shouting; then thunderous footsteps pounded the pavement in their direction. "Run! This way!" Angelo shouted. He grabbed Sara by the hand and pulled her down the alley to the right. It was only wide enough for them to go single-file. Angelo and Sara ducked into one of the houses, and he led her up toward the roof of the house. The rooftops were their own set of passageways with boards and sheet metal connecting the homes into an elaborate system. They continued to run on the rooftops until someone spotted them from below, and they were ducking bullets once more. They went back down to the street, but Sara was out of breath, and her side ached from running.

"If we stay here, they're going to find us, and they will kill us for sure," Angelo warned. "We have to go." Sara winced with pain as they began running again, twisting through the alleys and dodging bullets. They finally made it to the border, and Angelo stopped.

"Go! Don't look back; keep going. I'm going to lead them away." Angelo said. Before she could object, Angelo was running again. Sara continued running until she saw a taxi.

"I need to get to the Hilton Barra Hotel, please. I can pay you when we get there; just drive quickly, please." The cab driver nodded and pressed his foot to the gas. The farther they got from the favela, the safer Sara felt, but she couldn't help thinking of Angelo. She hoped that he escaped too.

When she got to the hotel, a man in a black suit was waiting for her. "Sara Jensen?" He asked.

"Yes," Sara said apprehensively. *What if this is one of them? What if they have come to kill me?* The worst thoughts went through her head, and she froze. "It's okay; I'm from the consulate." He told her, sensing her trepidation. Sara breathed a sigh of relief as the man pulled out his phone. "Dunn? Yeah, I got her. She came back to the hotel. Yes, oh, wow. Okay, I will let her know." From the one-sided conversation, Sara knew that Dunn had stumbled onto something.

"What is it? Are they okay?" Sara asked.

"They're fine. Dunn and Charlotte located Henry, but he was very ill. They wanted to take him to the hospital, but he keeps asking for a priest. They're headed to a Catholic church here in town. I can drive you."

"I have to get some money from my room to pay the cab driver," Sara told him.

"Don't worry about it. I got it." They went outside to where the cab driver was waiting. The man handed him a few notes, and the driver's eyes widened. "Thank you for your patience." He said.

"No problem at all, thank you!" The cab pulled away, and Sara could see the grin on the driver's face even as he drove from the lot. "Something tells me that was the most generous tip he's been given all day," Sara said. "You know me, but I don't know you, and if I'm honest, running off with strangers hasn't turned out so well as of late. What's your name?" Sara asked.

"I'm Frank. We have to hurry." Frank led her to his black SUV. Frank was middle-aged. Sara could tell from the salt and pepper color of his hair. He proudly displayed a thick, gold wedding band on his finger.

"Do you and your wife have kids?" Sara asked.

"We do. Two girls and a boy." Frank said.

"Do they live here in Rio?"

"Yes. We have lived here for about five years now. We moved here from Sao Paulo."

"Do you ever worry about their safety here? I mean, I have only been here for a week or so, and already I have seen my friend murdered, I've been kidnapped, shot at, and chased through the streets."

"Well, our first rule is; don't go to the favelas. I also have a bodyguard to accompany my wife and kids when they go out. That's more to prevent them from being robbed. They don't do drugs or buy guns, so they stay very much off the radar of the local gangs."

"That's what I should have done," Sara said.

Frank stopped the car in front of the largest church Sara had ever seen. The stonework arches on the front of the building rivaled the statue of Christ the Redeemer. The stained glass windows were enormous and beautifully crafted mosaics of Jesus, Mary, and the cross. Sara was in awe.

Dunn was waiting for them just inside the doors; he thanked Frank and shook his hand.

"Stay safe, Sara," Frank said.

Dunn led Sara to the basement. "Is Henry down here?"

"He is, but I have to prepare you. This is how we found him." Dunn took out his phone and showed Sara the pictures. Henry was crumpled on the floor with his back arched like a serpent. All around him, the walls were covered in writing—one word, written in blood. *Confess*. It was like the past had come back.

"This is just like what happened to Stacy, and you remember her hovering above her cot in that footage I showed you from her cell, right? Can you still deny that maybe it's something supernatural? How can someone who has had no sign of mental illness in the past have the same symptoms as another without ever seeing it for himself?"

"Syphilitic insanity?" Dunn joked. When he saw Sara's unamused expression, his smile disappeared.

"Look, If you had told me a year ago that a suspect was possessed and that I would be in Brazil witnessing the exorcism of that suspect, I would have sent you to the loony bin myself, but here we are. The priests believe he is possessed, you do too, and I have no evidence to disprove your theory, so it doesn't matter what I think; this is the reality of the situation. Suddenly the basement was filled with a loud metallic banging. Dunn rushed down the hall and around the corner. Sara followed him into a large room where three priests had strapped Henry to a metal table. Henry thrashed and fought. He screamed obscenities at the priests and spit at them. The priest on his right side had a thurible; a cloud of thick smoke poured out from the holes in the sides. He swung it back and forth over Henry's body. It smelled like sage to Sara, and she knew that often people would use it to cleanse spirits from a house, so why not a body?

The priest on the left of Henry was splashing him with holy water. The priest in the middle read passages from the bible. Henry fought against them, contorting his body into inhuman shapes. Strong leather bonds held him to the table in a flayed position as his bones cracked and bent.

"Get out! Get out! You will leave this vessel, which is a vessel of God; in his name, I Order you. Get out!" The priests began chanting together. The priest in the center held up his crucifix and touched it to Henry's forehead as they chanted. Henry cried as his mind took control of his body once more. He fell limp against the table.

"I don't have the strength to keep fighting it." Henry cried. The entity within him took hold once more, and Henry started choking. His eyes bulged like something was strangling him, and the fingertip-shaped bruises appeared on his neck before their eyes. Charlotte screamed and ran from the basement, her feet echoing through the stone hall. Henry's back arched, and the entire table lifted from the floor. The three priests all jumped on it at once, pushing it back down, they continued their assault on the spirit.

Sara was horrified, but she couldn't look away. The priests continued chanting and dousing Henry with holy water, showing him the crucifix, and reading passages from the bible. Each time they thought they were making progress, Henry would writhe in pain from the entity inside him. Finally, Henry slept. His breathing was fast and came out in short grunts. His eyes fluttered inside his eyelids.

"Is it over?" Sara asked. One of the priests turned around to face her.

"No, it could be hours, or even days, depending on how deep the spirit or demon has rooted itself into the host." Sara sat down in the corner. Dunn followed and sat beside her.

"You okay?" He asked.

"Are *you?* I mean, here we are, witnessing the existence of life after death, good and evil, and the power of God. I grew up in a Baptist church. My great grandfather, grandfather, great uncle, and father were all Baptist pastors. My mother abused me; we later discovered she was mentally ill and had her committed, but not before she destroyed my faith. I prayed to God to save me from her for years, and when it didn't happen and the abuse continued and got worse, I questioned how a loving and merciful God could allow a child to endure such torture. Then I thought that maybe he just didn't care about me, specifically. I was almost a teenager when I decided that God didn't exist.

I convinced myself that God and the idea of heaven was a fairy tale that people throughout history used as a tactic to get others to give them their money, or to lead good lives, or to get children to obey their parents, or wives their husbands." Sara rested her forehead on her arms, which she folded across her knees. Dunn put a comforting hand on her back.

"If you're okay, I'm going to go upstairs and check on Charlotte," Dunn said. Standing to his feet. "You want to come with?" He asked, suddenly feeling insensitive.

"No, I'm okay. I just need a little while to myself. Would you mind if I used your phone?" She asked before he left.

"not at all." Dunn handed her his cell phone and walked down the hall and up the stairs. When he was gone, Sara called Angelo, thankful for her eidetic memory for phone numbers, now more than ever. Someone answered, but it was not Angelo. It was a gruff-sounding man who spoke in Portuguese. Sara hung up. A feeling of dread washed over her, and she ran upstairs to Dunn.

"They captured Angelo." She announced.

"What? Who did?" Dunn asked.

"The Red Order, the gang that controls Complexo do Alemão. They had us both, but Angelo helped me escape. We have to get him back." Sara said.

"Are you crazy? We can't take on an entire gang to save one man." Dunn said.

"Then we get reinforcements. Maybe we could convince the Brazilian government to attempt pacification?" Sara suggested.

"Pacification is dangerous, not only for the officers and the gang members but the innocent civilians as well. You don't realize what you're asking."

"I do. I'm asking you to try and help me save my friend."

"What about Henry? What if this is successful, and we need to get him back to the states quickly. We didn't come here to start a war in Brazil, and that's what pacification is; it's war." Sara had never seen Dunn so angry.

"I wouldn't mind taking out a few of the assholes responsible for Kristofer's death." Charlotte smiled for the first time in a week, and it was a sinister smile, filled with the lust for revenge.

"One thing at a time, we have to be here for Henry now. You know, the job we are being paid to do." That was the end of the conversation; Dunn would hear no more about pacification or daring rescues.

The three of them walked back downstairs to find the priests praying over Henry once more. He wasn't fighting this time. Instead, he was grunting and breathing as if he were trying to awaken from a nightmare. His skin was gray and seemed like it was dying on his body. He had cuts, scratches, and bruises all over.

One of the priests blessed Henry and poured the holy water on his head.

"In the name of the father, the son, and the holy spirit, I order you to leave this vessel of God. God Orders you to leave his child." Henry started contorting again as another priest placed the crucifix on his chest. It seared into his skin, and he screamed in pain, using a voice that wasn't his; it was a woman's voice, deep and angry.

"CONFESS," it screamed, "CONFESS!" The table began to shake and, despite its size and weight, went flying across the room with Henry still strapped to it. It toppled over, smashing Henry beneath it. Everyone watched in shock as Henry lifted the table with his back and stood on his feet, screaming at them.

The priests rushed over and pushed the table back down. Henry was able to break one of the leather straps holding his arm and backhanded the priest that happened to be next to it. The priest flew backward into the stone wall, and a sickening crack echoed through the basement as his head met with the brick. He slid down the wall, streaking blood to the floor, his eyes still wide with shock even though his body lay lifeless.

Henry began laughing as he reached for the strap holding his other arm.

"Help us. Quickly!" a priest screamed, looking toward Dunn. Dunn rushed up to hold down Henry's free arm while the priests replaced the broken strap with another. Henry fought against it, thrashing wildly and bucking his body, which was more thin and frail than it had been the last time Dunn saw him at his house. When they had Henry strapped back down, Dunn released him and stepped back to let the priests continue.

Hours passed, and it finally seemed like Henry was free. He understood questions and Orders, he could nod his head, but he didn't speak. Dunn thought it might be due to shock. He had just been through the most horrible ordeal that Dunn had ever seen.

"We will leave him strapped down for at least twenty-four hours. If the spirit is still within him, it will manifest again within that time. You should get some rest, and we need to take care of Father Neumann. They began to move Father Neumann's body, and Dunn started to object. "It's okay, sir; we take care of our own when something happens during an exorcism. There is no way to explain what happened here to the police. We will notify his family, and the church will pay for his funeral." Dunn nodded and led Charlotte and Sara from the basement and back to the van.

"I believe there is one other way that we can rescue Angelo," Sara said as they got into the van.

"You aren't going to give up on this, are you?" Dunn asked.

"I can't. Angelo helped me escape, The gang that took us knew I was a cop, and they would have killed me. He's my friend, and I can't abandon him." She said. "The warehouse where they kept me is in the north of the favela. They might have taken him back there; it seems to be a kind of hideout for them. If I see it from above, I can point it out. I say we ride the cable car. I will point out the warehouse, and then we can get there from the top of the hill, which will be easier and shorter than coming from the city border. I know how to get onto the roof, and I can crawl through the vent systems like we did when I escaped the first time, but I will need a distraction. That's where you come in. We will need firecrackers and lots of them. You two will need to set them off around town to incite panic and make the gang members think they are under attack by a rival gang. Once they take off in the other direction, I can climb onto the roof. I will find Angelo and get him to the roof. Have the consulate send a helicopter on my signal and extract us."

"That's a dangerous plan for all involved, and we only have 24 hours to pull it off. Where can we buy firecrackers?" Dunn asked.

"I saw a fireworks store the night we went for our first drive around the city," Charlotte said. "We can take a taxi; they will know how to get there." She suggested.

# CHAPTER THIRTY

The preparation took more time than they had expected, and it was nearing evening by the time they got ready to set their plan into action. The helicopter was on standby, Sara was once again wearing a wire, and she replaced the cell phone the gang had taken from her when they took her captive. Dunn connected the firecrackers to timed detonators, and a few of Dunn's friends from the consulate offered to help place them around the favela.

They positioned the decoys near the warehouse but far enough away that it would draw them out. As the red Order filed out of the warehouse, the decoy gunfire spread farther away, leading them on a goose chase through the labyrinth of alleyways. Sara climbed the truck that was still parked on the backside of the building and pulled herself onto the roof. She opened the vent and lowered herself gently into the duct system.

Sara crawled back down the slope and turned left at the cross-section. The grates all looked down on empty rooms. *So far, so good.* Sara thought. She crawled back to the grate over the room that she was sure they were held captive in last time and opened the latch. Sara used the shelf to climb down and looked around for Angelo. He wasn't there. Sara cracked the door open and peeked out into the hallway in both directions. She listened at each door before poking her head inside to look for Angelo. Finally, she found him, tied to a chair, and beaten. Even through the blindfold, Sara could see the swelling of his eyes.

Sara rushed to the center of the room and began untying Angelo's bonds. "Sara? Is that you?" He asked.

"Yes, it's me; we have to hurry!" Sara's voice was no more than a whisper as she loosened the ropes. Just as Angelo stood up from his chair, the door to the room slammed shut. Sara jumped and turned toward the noise to see a man in a black tank top, jean shorts, and a balaclava pointing an assault rifle at them. He spoke in Portuguese.

"He says that they knew you'd come back for me and that you have seen too many of their faces to be allowed to leave but..." His voice trailed off. "No, please." He begged.

"What?" Sara asked. "What else did he say?" She began to cry.

"He said you're too pretty to kill, at least before they've passed you around." Sara looked at the man in disgust. She spat at his feet. The man lunged forward and backhanded her hard across the face. Although Angelo's eyes were swollen, almost entirely closed, he tried to push the guy away from Sara. Angelo took another hit, this time in the jaw, and he fell to the floor.

The man must have thought he knocked him unconscious because he laid down his rifle and grappled Sara, wrestling her to the floor and forcing himself on top of her. Sara felt the man's sweat dripping on her as he reached for the button on her shorts, tearing at her clothes like a wild animal. He was so preoccupied; the gangster didn't notice Angelo grab the gun from the floor beside him and jump to his feet in one swift move. Angelo swung it by the barrel, and it made a loud thwack as it connected with the man's skull.

Angelo strapped the rifle over his shoulder and helped Sara to her feet.

"Are you okay?" He asked. Sara threw her arms around him in relief and joy.

"I'm okay, but we have to go." She pulled out her phone, sent the coordinates to the helicopter, and they made their way to the roof. Angelo unloaded the rifle and threw the ammunition off the roof and left the gun at his feet.

The helicopter hovered over the building and dropped the ladder. Sara climbed up first, and then Angelo. The aircraft drew the attention of everyone in town as they knew it would, and Sara heard the deafening ping ping ping of bullets hitting the helicopter from below.

They were soon lifting off, and Sara breathed a sigh of relief as they left the range of gunfire.

"Angelo needs a doctor and maybe some x-rays. Can we land at the hospital?" She asked. The pilot used the radio to call the hospital for permission to land, and they granted it. Once Angelo was admitted, Dunn and Charlotte were ready to head back to the church to check on Henry. Sara looked conflicted between her job and not wanting to leave until she knew Angelo would be okay.

"It's okay, Sara. You stay with Angelo, we can handle Henry, and the US Marshall is ready for our call so that we will have plenty of help." Dunn told her. She hugged them both and watched as they left, and then sat down in the waiting room. She fell asleep for a while, maybe hours, and woke up to Angelo's doctor quietly saying her name.

"Ms. Jensen?" Sara nodded and waited for the doctor to continue. "Angelo is out of surgery. We had to put a plate in his left cheek beside his eye socket to keep it from collapsing. He has some broken ribs and had some internal bleeding, which we were able to get under control. He's heavily sedated now for pain, but if you want, you can sit with him in his room." Sara stood and followed the doctor.

The swelling in Angelo's eyes was already starting to look better, and his bruises were turning green. He was sleeping, but Sara still went to his bedside and sat in the recliner next to him.

"Let us know if there is anything you need." The doctor said, and shortly after, his footsteps were receding down the hall.

Sara took Angelo's hand in hers. "Thank you. You saved my life not once, or even twice, but three times. I can never repay you." Sara felt his fingers tighten ever so slightly around hers, and she knew that he heard her. She smiled and fell asleep in the chair beside him.

# CHAPTER THIRTY-ONE

Sara was awakened the next morning by Angelo's nurse when she came in to take his vitals. She made sure that his pain was still managed for the time being but lowered his dose of the morphine drip. The nurse spoke to him in Portuguese, and Shelby was all that Sara understood, and Sara knew that it was her name. Sara asked her if she spoke English and was pleasantly surprised that she did.

"Were your parents a fan of the Mustang?" Sara asked.

"No, my dad was just in that movie about the mustang back in seventy-three, well, it came out in seventy-four I think, anyway, he wanted to name me Elanor, but my mom said that it sounded too old-fashioned. He settled for Shelby."

"I like that name, and it was a great mustang too!" Sara smiled at her, and she seemed to return it as she went about her work.

Shelby made sure that Angelo had the call button if he needed anything, and then she went on to her next patient. Angelo smiled at Sara.

"You're still here." He said. It wasn't a question, and he said it with such minimal surprise. "You better watch out; I might get the impression you like me or something."

"I can see they didn't break your sense of humor, just like twenty of your bones." Sara joked.

Angelo winced in pain as he tried to sit up. He reached for his water cup on his bedside table, but he couldn't quite get it. Sara stood up and positioned the tray over his bed so that he could reach everything on it.

"Thank you, Sara," Angelo said, looking into her eyes. He broke the gaze first, remembering that she had a boyfriend. They avoided the awkward silence because Dunn and Charlotte came into the room at that moment.

"How is he?" Charlotte asked.

"Better. The swelling has gone down a lot." Sara told them.

"The doctor should be by in a little while. The nurse told me they might release me today." Angelo said.

"That's great news, but where will you go? You can't go back to the favela." Sara said. Angelo's face fell as this was the first time he realized he would never get to see his dance students again.

"You're right. I'm not sure. I would have to get out of Rio altogether. I have a cousin in Sao Paulo, I could probably stay with him, but I don't have my car, or any money, or even anything I could sell to get money." Angelo said.

"Don't worry about that; you saved my life three times; I saved yours once; the way I see it, we're not even yet. We'll get you to Sao Paulo, and I will give you some money to get yourself on your feet there." Sara said. "That's three."

"You're such a good friend. I am happy I met you." Angelo said.

"Even if it completely changed your life, and maybe not for the better?" She asked.

"It was definitely for the better." Sara's cheeks flushed bright pink, and Angelo smiled. He had dimples that Sara thought were adorable and kind of made him look like Mario Lopez. She turned away before anyone realized that she was staring.

"How is Henry?" Sara asked, turning to Dunn.

"He seems okay now. He seems to be himself. The Marshall has him in custody, and their plane will be flying out tomorrow morning if he doesn't have another episode." Dunn said.

"I guess that means our time here is getting short," Sara said as she looked at Angelo.

"That's our cue," Dunn said, getting to his feet. He offered a hand to Charlotte, and she took it as she stood up. "I will see you later at the hotel," Dunn said to Sara. When all was quiet in the room, except for the occasional beep of the medical equipment, Sara scooted the chair to Angelo's bed.

"You know, when I tried to call you, and one of those guys answered your phone, I was so worried that they were going to kill you that I wouldn't make it to you in time. I hope that even when I have to leave to go back home, you'll keep in touch and promise me, you'll stay away from Alemão." Sara said.

"That's a hard thing to promise, but you know I value my life, so I think I can manage. I promise I won't go back there." Angelo smiled. "Thanks again for coming to rescue me. I didn't think I would ever see you again, but I'm glad I was wrong."

"Me too," she said. Sara laid her head on Angelo's chest, and he slid over in the bed to make room for her to snuggle beside him.


When the doctor came in around lunchtime, Sara stepped out into the hall so the doctor could look at Angelo. Sara went to the cafeteria and got a cup of coffee and a bagel. She passed by the emergency room on her way back up to Angelo's room, and there, waiting in the lobby, was the man Angelo had cracked in the head with his own rifle. He looked up and saw her. Sara started to back away as he stood up; his face flushed with anger as he started walking toward her. She turned and ran, spilling her coffee on the first step. Sara made it to the elevator and saw him running after her. The doors slid closed just in time, and she heard him bang on the doors as the elevator began to ascend. Sara pressed the number for the floor above Angelo's room to throw him off just in case.

When the elevator opened, she ran for the emergency stairwell and ran down the flight of stairs to Angelo's floor. Sara entered the room, covered in coffee and out of breath.

"What's wrong, Sara?" Angelo asked in alarm.

"He's here, the one who was guarding you. He was in the emergency room; he knows we're here." Sara explained. Sara stopped for a moment and looked at Angelo; he had gotten dressed in his clothes, which Dunn had been kind enough to have washed for him.

"The doctor is releasing me; I'm just waiting for paperwork," Angelo said.

"Good. I will call Dunn and get back up here so we can get out of here safely. Call the nurse and tell her you don't want any visitors. Except for Harold Dunn and Charlotte Bradley," Angelo did what Sara asked, and then, they waited. When Dunn arrived with a security detail from the consulate, Sara finally felt safe again. As they walked out under guard, Sara caught a glimpse of the man who chased her. Angelo saw him too. He pointed to Angelo and made a slicing motion across his throat with his thumb.

They set off immediately for Sao Paulo. Sara let Angelo use her phone to call his cousin to see if he could stay with him.

"Is it dangerous where he lives too?" Sara asked.

"No, He's a doctor. Back when he worked a labor job, he was injured while working. The company didn't have insurance for their employees, so he won an enormous settlement from them.

He used his settlement to get into the academy of plastic surgery. He has a nice place in the city."

"Good for him," Sara said. "Maybe he can help you start a dance studio. I am sure the kids of Sao Paulo would love a Latin hip hop dance class!"

"Maybe, We'll see. I can always work it off somehow."

Angelo turned and looked out the window of the SUV. He stared off into the horizon as they drove the coastline. Sara looked at him. She admired how the sun made his skin glow golden brown and how his eyes, which were deep brown, looked like chocolate. *Some girl is going to be very lucky to have him someday.* She thought, and then she turned her head and looked out the window on her side, thinking about going home. She thought about James and her job at the department; it all seemed like it would be so dull after this adventure.

Sara found herself wishing that she could stay in Brazil with Angelo, but she knew that it would seem much like her life at home after the danger was gone, but with a more scenic view.

They stopped for dinner and stretched their legs when they reached the halfway point in a run-down-looking little town off the highway. It wasn't much to see, but the small white brick restaurant had delicious food. Sara couldn't read the menu, so she let Angelo order for her, and he did not disappoint. After dinner, Angelo and Sara took a walk and came across a small botanical garden park. An elegant fountain decorated the middle of the square. On both sides of the brink walkway, all kinds of flowers brightened up the park. Fairy lights illuminated lilies, orchids, and enormous lilac bushes. Angelo stopped and turned to Sara.

"Hey, look, I know you have a boyfriend, but I have to tell you that despite our near-death experiences and running for our lives, the time I have shared with you, well, I'll never forget. We might never see each other again after tomorrow, so if I don't tell you how I feel about you now, I will regret it forever. I want to be with you. I don't know where we would live, we could figure it out, but I need you, Sara." Angelo leaned in but waited for Sara to meet him in the middle, which she did without hesitation. The world seemed to stop around them, and all they could feel was the spark between them. Their kiss deepened, and Sara felt weightless as her heart soared. When Angelo finally let her go, her face tingled more than it ever had, and she knew her cheeks had turned a bright red. "I'll be devastated if you leave."

"Me too," Sara admitted.

"They headed back to the vehicle where They saw Charlotte and Dunn chatting while they waited.

"You guys ready?" Charlotte asked. Sara nodded and got into the car silently as Anglo's words replayed in her head. She could still feel his lips on hers, and it made her heart ache. When they looked at each other, she could see that he felt it too. *It's just not fair. Why couldn't I have met him first?*

Sara was angry at herself for feeling this way. The next three hours seemed to pass by too quickly, and before she knew it, Dunn was pulling up in front of a beautiful house in Sao Paulo.

"This is it." Dunn said, and the GPS agreed as it rang out, "You have arrived."

Sara walked Angelo to the door and hugged him before he rang the bell. When his cousin opened the door and hugged Angelo, Sara backed away as they started to talk. Angelo saw her backing up and stopped her.

"Wait, Sara, I want you to meet my cousin, Julien Rodrigo; Julien, this is Sara, she saved my life." Angelo looked at her with admiration as Julien shook her hand.

"It's wonderful to meet you. Thank you for rescuing my cousin." He turned to Angelo. "I will go make up the guest room upstairs so you two can say goodbye." Angelo gently grabbed his arm to stop him and leaned in to whisper in his ear. "Of course. Minha casa e sua casa." Julien told him.

After Julien was back inside the house, Sara looked at Angelo. `"What did you ask him?"

"I asked him if I could convince you to stay with me; if you could stay here too. He said, of course, and that his house is my house. You don't *have* to leave; you could choose me. We have something here- I know it." He gestured between them. Sara looked back to the SUV where Dunn and Charlotte were waiting; then, she looked back at Angelo.

His eyes sparkled as he looked at her, and she felt weak. No one had ever made her feel like this before. Sara felt a knot the size of a boulder in her stomach at the thought of returning home. Sara walked back to the car.

"Our tickets are open-ended. Meaning I could leave tomorrow?" Dun smiled and nodded.

"You can come home whenever you'd like." He said. "I bought our tickets, not the department, so it's here for you whenever you're ready. I'll email it to you." Sara smiled at him. He stepped out of the car to hug her, and Charlotte did the same.

"Take care of this guy for me, will you?" Sara whispered to Charlotte and gestured to Dunn.

"You say that like you're not coming back at all." Sara looked at her and shrugged, then returned to Angelo's side, waving to her friends as they left for the airport.

# CHAPTER THIRTY-TWO

When Dunn and Charlotte arrived back in the USA, it was late. "Where are you staying tonight?" Dunn asked, looking at Charlotte.

"I guess I'm going to check into a hotel." She said.

"That would be a waste unless you get more than one day, and then you'd have to wake up early too. Why don't you just come to stay at my place? You can take the bed, and I will pull out the couch." Dunn offered. "Then you can sleep as long as you'd like." He added.

"That sounds nice." Dunn helped carry her bags to his car, which was not as impressive as the SUV they had gotten to drive in Rio, but it was spacious enough for the two of them. The parking fee was outrageous, but thank goodness for the department funding they received. Dunn swiped the visa with the department funds on it, and the gate lifted.

When they got back to Dunn's apartment, He carried Charlotte's bags in for her and then turned down the bed. He gave her the remote control and then went over to pull out the hide-a-bed inside his love seat. They said goodnight to each other and then slept for the next eighteen hours. They woke up to Dunn's phone, ringing loudly. He groaned and rolled over to answer it. He sat up urgently and began dressing, still holding the phone to his ear. "I'll be right in." He said. Charlotte looked at him with a worried expression.

"Henry's trial has been moved up. It's tomorrow morning. I need to go in and prepare. You're welcome to stay here, or I can drive you to your car if you want to leave." Dunn said.

"I think I will stick around. I want to go with you to the trial tomorrow." She said.

"Okay, sounds good. I'll see you in a little while." Dunn said. When he was gone, Charlotte ordered some food and had it delivered. She used the GPS on her phone to determine the delivery address.

When Dunn got to his desk, he immediately called Dr. Grant Hudson. "Hey, I know it's late, and I'm sorry to have to ask this, but could you possibly come and evaluate Henry's mental ability to stand trial? It's tomorrow, and I just need to make sure we get all the bases covered. I know the defense will have another doctor do it too; I just want to see if the reports are the same." He asked. Grant told him that he would be there within the hour. Dunn continued making his witness list and gathering his evidence to submit, although, with Henry's confession, he doubted that he would need it. Dunn went to see Henry before Dr. Hudson arrived. Henry didn't look well. His eyes were dark and heavy; his skin was pale and stretched tightly across his bones. Dunn tried to catch his eye, but it was like Henry was staring right through him.

"Mr. Warren, Can you hear me?" Dunn asked. Henry only stared. Dunn nodded to the jailer to open his cell. Dunn walked over to where Henry was sitting and reached out to touch his shoulder. "Henry?"

A long low, hissing sound escaped Henry's throat as he turned his head slowly to look at Dunn.

"Henry's not here." The voice hissed. Henry's face looked alien and strange as his pupils enlarged, even more, turning his eyes completely black. Dunn looked at him in horror but tried not to lose his composure.

"If you're not Henry, who are you?" Henry started laughing; it sounded as if it were coming from deep inside him and echoed through the room. Dun felt uneasy as he began backing out of the cell. Henry continued to stare. Dunn turned to run as soon as he was outside the cell and bumped right into Grant. He let out a grunt as their chests collided, and Grant reached out and grabbed Dunn's arm before he could fly backward.

"Everything alright?" Grant asked.

"No, I would wait, don't go in there. Henry is possessed. I know how it sounds, but you didn't see what I saw in Brazil. The priests tried to perform an exorcism, but it didn't work." Dunn's voice was almost a whisper as he told Grant the story.

"It sounds like to me that he is suffering delusions and would benefit from a psychiatric evaluation. If you want him fit to stand trial, I should assess the situation as soon as possible." Grant started toward the cell.

"Okay, if you're going in there, I am going too, just in case you need backup. I will wait outside the cell." Grant nodded and clapped Dunn on the shoulder.

"Okay, I'll yell if I need you." Grant walked to Henry's cell, and the jailer opened it, then closed it behind him.

"Henry. I'm Dr. Hudson. Can I ask you a few questions?" Grant walked cautiously into the cell. When Henry heard his voice, he looked at him immediately; his gaze was hopeful.

Grant noticed that his eyes were the same as Verona's; after all, he was her father.

"Grant," Henry said.

"I don't recall telling you my first name." Henry looked at the floor. When he looked back up, a tear was running down his cheek.

"Henry, Why did you feel you needed an Exorcism?"

His eyes flashed in anger. "He didn't want to confess, he tried to run, but he couldn't run from me."

"Who are you?" Grant asked, inching closer.

"You don't recognize me?" Henry stood with his arms stretched open. "Maybe you just need to feel me again." Henry lunged at Grant, and before he could call out to Dunn, Henry's eyes rolled back into his head, and a swirling black mist escaped through Henry's mouth. Grant tried to scream, but the black smoke entered his mouth and clogged his throat. The choking feeling passed quickly enough, and Grant looked around, con-fused. Henry lay on the ground before him. Dunn came rushing in, "What happened?" Dunn asked.

"He fainted," Grant said. "Help me get him up?"

Dunn bent down to help Henry up off the floor. Grant put Henry's arm over his shoulder, and they walked him to his cot. Henry was waking up now. *His eyes are different now.* Grant thought as he looked at Henry. Henry's eyes, just moments ago, had been identical to Verona's, blue and deep. Now their shape was slanted downward, and his eyes were darker, hazel instead of blue.

"Henry, can you hear me? Do you remember who I am?" Grant asked. Henry shook his head.

"Do you remember why you're here?"

"Because of Verona, I helped cover for Stacy." Henry started to cry.

"I would say he will be okay to stand trial tomorrow; he just needs some rest. I will come by in the morning to talk to him again; what time is the trial?"

"I think nine-thirty," Dunn said. "I will confirm and text you." Grant nodded.

The next morning, Dunn received a call from the night-shift guard in charge of Henry.

"You told me to call if there were any changes in Mr. Warren. He's eating again. He had not eaten a bite since he was brought in until last night after you and Dr. Hudson left. He asked for food, and we had a meal brought in. He devoured it. I have never seen a man so hungry. This morning, we brought breakfast, dropped his tray off first, and by the time we had delivered the other inmates' food, he had finished and was asking for more. We had an extra tray, so we gave it to him, and he ate that too. He is looking a lot better now; it's the strangest thing."

"Okay, Thanks for calling." *This is good news*, Dunn thought.

# CHAPTER THIRTY-THREE

Grant felt hands trailing down his chest when he woke. He didn't open his eyes; Grant just laid there and enjoyed the light touch. Then, Grant felt a hot breath on his neck, followed by kisses. He moaned but didn't move. He was enjoying this. The kisses moved from his neck to his chest, and his back arched as the kisses went lower still, and arousal consumed him. He moaned Iris' name and tried to put his arms around his surprise lover, and that's when he found himself not able to move. He was paralyzed. He was able to open his eyes, though, and he saw Verona's face staring back at him, only it was an angry version of her that he had never seen before.

"Don't you see? We can still be together." Verona scratched her nails down Grant's chest, and he cried out in pain. Grant tried to get up, but he couldn't, but he found that he could still speak.

"Alexa, Call Iris." He said. His phone lit up from the bedside table, and he could hear the faint ringing. When it stopped, and he heard Iris answer, he cried out.

"Help me!" He looked up at Verona, who looked angrier than ever. She drew back and slapped him across the face, hard. Her hand moved around his throat. He squeezed his eyes shut, hoping this was a nightmare from which he would awaken when he opened his eyes again.

"I just wanted us to be together. They took you away from me; they took our child; they had to pay. Why won't you look at me? LOOK!" Verona screamed. She straddled him, looking down at him the way she used to when they made love, but her expression was not as happy and soft as it was back then. Verona stroked the side of his face as she leaned down to press her lips to his. He froze with fear as Verona kissed him because he still couldn't move. Just then, Grant heard his front door open, and Iris called his name from down the hall.

"Who is this?" Verona looked at Grant, and then her head spun toward the door with a sickening crack. He could hear Iris's footsteps approaching. The bedroom door opened slowly, and as it did, the lamp on the bedside table flew across the room and shattered against the door frame.

"No!" Grant shouted. Verona disappeared, and the black mist entered Grant once more as his bedroom door swung open. Iris ran over to him as he sat up, coughing. Bruises began forming on his neck at the sides of his throat. They looked like fingerprints. Iris hugged him, and when she pulled back to look at him, she only saw the anger on his face. He reached out and tried to grab her by the neck, but she saw it coming and jumped back from him.

"Grant, What the hell is wrong with you?" She screamed as he stood up and stepped toward her. Iris backed away. Grant lunged forward to make a grab for her. Iris dodged, and Grant hit the door frame as Iris ran from the room. From deep inside himself, Grant fought the darkness that was trying to consume him. He scratched and clawed his way up from the dark hole that Verona buried him in.

"Wait. Help me!" He called. Iris turned and looked at him helplessly as some unseen force threw his body to the far end of the hall. Grant crashed against the shelf, and it crumbled under the power and weight of his body. Grant wasn't moving, and he slumped against the wall on top of the pile of broken shelving. Iris inched toward him.

"Grant, Are you okay?" He didn't move. Iris walked a little closer and called his name again. The lights above him flickered, and Iris swore she saw a shadow move up the hall toward her. Iris began to back away with her heart pounding in her chest as something took hold of her. She felt it enter her. Iris felt full and confused for a moment until she saw Grant move.

"Grant!" She called out as she heard him groan. Iris rushed over to his side. "Are you okay?" Grant opened his eyes to see Iris hovering over him. He smiled, relieved to see her unharmed.

"Thank God!" He said as he climbed to his feet. He embraced Iris and kissed her on the top of her head as he held her close. "I am so happy you're okay; I have no idea what's going on here or what just happened. I'm just glad it's over, and you're okay." He looked her up and down; her blue eyes sparkled down at him as he smiled at her and cupped the side of her face. *Wait, weren't her eyes green?* Grant thought. He pushed the idea out of his mind, sure that he just remembered wrong from all the stress. *That's all this was, hallucinations from stress.* Grant told himself, trying to justify what just happened.

Iris kissed him urgently, and she quickly tucked a finger into the waistband of his shorts that he had slept in and pulled him back to the bedroom. She took control of him in a way that made him feel excited; he couldn't resist her, even if he wanted to.

Hours later, they both lay exhausted and satisfied, wrapped in each other's arms.

Grant didn't realize what time it was until he heard his phone ringing.

"Hello?"

"Hey, where are you? Henry's hearing is about to start." Dunn said.

"Oh, I will be right there; I'm sorry, I had a rough morning."

Grant ended the call and quickly began dressing. He kissed Iris on his way out of the room. "Stay if you want, I will be back in a few hours." He smiled at her and left the room in a hurry.

Grant got to the courtroom just as the hearing was beginning. He sat down in the back so he wouldn't disturb the proceedings.

"Henry Warren, you have been charged with unlawful disposal of a corpse and obstruction of justice; how would you like to plead?" The judge asked.

Henry stood up and cleared his throat. He looked at the judge, and finally, he spoke.

"Guilty, your honor." He said. A sigh of relief flooded the prosecution side of the courtroom; there was no one on the defense side to object. Even Henry's court-appointed lawyer was not surprised by his plea.

"Given your plea of guilty, we are going to take a brief recess, and we will reconvene at eleven for sentencing." The judge said. He dismissed the jury, and Henry was escorted by two armed officers back to his holding cell.

"Not even Henry's wife, Madeline, came to support him," Henry said as he and Grant met outside the courtroom.

"Why would she? He is the reason she has no children left." Grant said.

"Want to grab a cup of coffee?" Dunn asked.

"Yes, *please!*" They left the courthouse and walked down the street a couple of blocks to a famous, locally-owned coffee shop.

They ordered and then sat at a table in the back of the room. Neither Grant nor Dunn talked; they both zoned out until a waitress sat their drinks in front of them. They both thanked her, and when she was far enough away not to overhear, Grant finally spoke.

"So, last night, you mentioned what you saw in Brazil. Something about Henry being possessed?" Grant asked.

"I saw the priests trying to perform an exorcism, and I saw things I can't explain, like steel tables flying across a room or super-human strength. Whatever it was, it wasn't Henry, and it got angry when the priests tried to expel it. It even killed one of them, threw him against the wall so hard that his head smashed in." Dunn sipped his coffee, and as he set the cup down on the saucer, Grant could see that his hands were shaking.

"Let's say he was *possessed*. Why did they let him leave if the exorcism wasn't successful?" Grant asked.

"They had to sedate him. They did all that they could. They thought, at the very least, they brought Henry back into the forefront of his consciousness. Henry was in control again, and they sedated him to keep it that way until we got him back here. The marshal who accompanied him back had to administer a second dose." Dunn told him.

"Did the priests happen to say how this entity came to possess Henry?"

"They said that the spirit's hold on Henry was strong because they might have had a strong bond in life."

Grant suddenly felt very worried about Iris. He couldn't tell Dunn what had happened; he wasn't sure he believed it himself.

"Will you excuse me a moment? I have to make a call." Grant got up and walked to the quiet corner by the bathroom hall. He dialed Iris's number. He was relieved and thankful that she answered.

"How's the morning errand going?"

"Not bad; I just wanted to check in on you."

"I'm okay, I went out to run some errands of my own, but I'd love to have dinner together tonight. Let's say, at eight pm at Bistro?"

"Sounds Great. See you then." Grant said.

"Love you!" Iris said these words as naturally as she said hello, even though they had only been dating for a few weeks and they had not yet said this to each other. Grant thought it was odd and was grateful that Iris ended the call without expecting him to say it back. *Perhaps it was just a slip of the tongue?* Grant thought to himself. He tried not to think about it, but the more he tried, the more he failed. Grant liked Iris a lot, but this morning had been their first time being intimate, and then she had said those two words so casually. These events followed the incident that happened this morning with Verona. Had it been a nightmare or a hallucination? Grant wasn't sure, but he felt uneasy, so much so that he jumped when Dunn came up and clapped him on the shoulder.

"Everything okay?" He asked, concerned.

"Yeah, sorry, just a little jumpy. I had a nightmare this morning that kind of rattled me. I guess I am just still thinking about it."

"What do you think that means, Doc? You are the expert on that kind of thing." Dunn asked.

"Not sure, stress maybe? I'm still grieving, I know because I'm seeing Verona." Dunn's expression turned from concern to fear as he pieced together events in his head.

"Remember when you talked to Henry?" Dunn held up a finger to let Grant know he was on a train of thought and Grant shouldn't derail it. Grant nodded and listened. "Well, after you left, Henry was more himself; he ate and talked. Henry admitted to the guard that he didn't remember how he got there or what happened before taking him into custody. The last thing he remembered was fleeing to Brazil because they wouldn't extradite him. Then he said everything went dark like he was buried alive and he has no memories from that time." Grant remembered that same feeling when Iris was leaving. She had been scared, but he didn't remember what made her feel that way. Dunn continued.

"What if- now I know how this is going to sound, but, what if the dark spirit he was trying to get rid of was Verona? She was obviously in love with you, so when you came in to talk to Henry, she saw the chance to be with you instead. Do you feel different since you talked to Henry?"

Grant got a sinking feeling in the pit of his stomach. The room was swirling around him. There was no medical explanation that could debunk what Dunn was saying and what had happened at his house this morning only reinforced this idea of possession. Grant had to sit down; his face was pale.

"In my nightmare, she said that we could still be together, then Iris walked in, and I felt anger within me, but it wasn't mine. Iris ran from the room. I remember following after her and begging her to help me. Then something pushed me. I broke a shelf when something threw me into it and passed out. When I woke up, Iris was standing over me, asking if I was okay. I saw her face though, before, when she was running away, she had been terrified of me, like I did something that I don't remember doing, but moments later, she was helping me to my feet and leading me back to bed." Grant suddenly thought of Iris's eyes looking down at him, her blue eyes, *Verona's blue eyes.*

Grant took out his phone and looked back through his photos. He found a picture of him and Iris from the night they went dancing. He looked at her eyes, her beautiful, *green* eyes.

"Let me know how the sentencing goes; I have to find Iris," Grant said. Dunn nodded and watched as Grant hurried out of the coffee shop.

# CHAPTER THIRTY-FOUR

Adam Sheffield was reading over a case file when he heard a pounding on his door. He groaned at the interruption and got up to see who was out there. He was surprised to see Grant looking very impatient and nervous. Adam opened the door quickly to let him inside. "What's going on, Grant? Is everything okay?"

"No, I really need a friend right now because what I am about to say is going to sound like I am crazy, and for fuck's sake, maybe I am, but there is too much shit going on that I just can't explain away with medicine, science, or diagnoses."

"Let's go sit down." He led Grant to the living room. "Would you like a drink? I have whiskey. It looks like you could use it." Adam pointed to Grant's shaking hand and his bouncing leg. Grant tried to steady himself, but he couldn't.

"Yes, please." He said, and Adam went to make them both a drink. Grant took some deep breaths and tried to meditate. *Adam is going to think I've lost it.* He thought. Grant heard Adam coming back and held down his legs to stop them from bouncing, but it started again as he reached up to take the glass from Adam.

"Now, what's going on?" Adam sat down on the love seat across from Grant.

"I'm a Psychiatrist, so I know how this sounds, but I think Verona's ghost is haunting me." Adam was careful not to react.

"What makes you say that?"

"I saw her; She was right in front of my face, then I felt *different*. Like she took control of me. Then Iris came in, and I blacked out."

"Is Iris okay?" Adam asked.

"I think so, only..." His voice trailed off as he took a deep, shaking breath. "Only, I don't think she is herself right now. I think Verona's spirit is possessing her."

Adam remembered that morning, or was it evening? He couldn't really remember because he had been drunk at the time, but he remembered seeing Verona. Adam recalled the way that the lights had flickered and then burst. He remembered how she had reached out to him and how he had felt afterward. Full. He felt full. What had happened next? Adam thought about it, and suddenly he remembered that he had woken up in the hospital.

They told him he had fainted. Grant's story sounded like the plot of a low-budget indie horror film, but a part of him had to believe it because he had seen it for himself.

"Say you're right, and that Verona *is* possessing Iris, how could we prove it, and who on earth would we have to prove it to?" Adam asked.

"Officer Dunn. He saw Brazilian priests try to perform an exorcism on Henry." Grant said. His leg was still bouncing as he downed his glass of whiskey. "We will need all the help we can get. I just want Iris to be okay." Grant looked desperate.

"Okay, I will get my things," Adam said.

Moments later, they were in Adam's car.

"Dunn should be leaving the courthouse as soon as Henry's sentencing is over; we could wait for him there," Grant suggested as Adam's engine roared to life.

"Sounds like a plan." Adam pulled away from the curb, and they were on their way.

"How do you think Verona would feel seeing the two of us together?" Adam asked with a smirk.

"Kinda like we're staging an intervention." Grant's expression relaxed just a little with this hint of humor.

When they arrived at the courthouse, Adam and Grant went inside and waited in the lobby. They spotted Dunn in the crowd as the courtroom emptied. Dunn knew, when they approached, that something was wrong.

"Remember what we talked about this morning at the coffee shop?" Grant asked. Dunn nodded and waited for Grant to continue. "We need to discuss it further, but not here. Can we go somewhere private?"

The three of them went to Grant's house together. He re-enacted the events that took place there that morning, and the other two watched him in shock as he described what he saw and the wreckage that followed.

"I think Verona's spirit is inside Iris now. Iris has green eyes, see?" He pulled out his phone and showed them the photo.

"This morning, she had blue eyes; they looked just like Verona's."

"When Henry was possessed, he didn't eat. Not even a single bite. He had no interest in food." Dunn said.

"She invited me to dinner tonight," Grant said, visibly confused.

"See if she eats, if she does, then Iris is probably not possessed, but if she doesn't..." Adam's voice faded as he shrugged his shoulders and left the others to speculate the end of the sentence.

"We need to find a priest here that does exorcism. I heard about a priest in Ohio who was trained by the Vatican to perform them." Dunn said. "I have been researching since I got back from Brazil. I will reach out and see if I can get him to come. I will find a location, and all you have to do is bring Iris there." Dunn pulled out his phone and started typing.

"So what do I do for now?" Grant asked.

"Pretend you suspect nothing. Spend time with Iris like normal. We can't let her get suspicious." Dunn told him.

Grant sat down, his leg bouncing more than ever. "I don't know if I can do it, just pretend that I'm not terrified. I mean, a week ago, I would have said that ghosts aren't real and that someone who was seeing ghosts was suffering delusions, but Adam and I have both seen Verona since she died."

"I saw Milan too. Remember that evening at the lake when I thought she was trapped under the ice and calling for help? Maybe I am delusional." Adam said.

Grant crossed the room to the bar. He grabbed a bottle of whiskey and three glasses. The three of them drank and made plans until the sun began to shine into the west-facing window, indicating that evening had arrived.

"It's almost time for me to meet Iris." It was evident that despite nearly finishing a bottle of whiskey between the three of them, that Grant was still nervous. "You guys can stay here; help yourselves." He gestured to the bar.

After Grant had showered and brushed his teeth to minimize the smell of whiskey, he called an Uber to take him to the restaurant.

Iris was already seated when Grant arrived. She stood when he approached and kissed his cheek before he sat down. The waitress brought them each a menu and took their drink order.

"I'm fine with water," Iris said.

"I'll have an unsweetened iced tea, please."

The waitress looked at Iris. "Are we ready to order, or do we need a few minutes?" She asked, noticing that Iris had not even moved to open her menu.

"I think we will need a few minutes," Grant said.

"Okay, I will be right back with your drinks." The waitress said and walked away from their table.

"Don't you need to look at the menu?" Grant asked as he read through the items on his menu.

"No, I'm not hungry. I'm just here for the company." Iris smiled at Grant, and her blue eyes made him uncomfortable. He shifted in his seat as the waitress returned with their drinks. She took the order pad out of her apron pocket.

"Do you know what you would like to eat?" She asked again.

"Sure. I'll have the blackened chicken salad with avocado and the jalapeno ranch dressing." Grant closed his menu and passed it back to the waitress. She looked at Iris.

"And what are you having tonight?"

"Oh, nothing for me, thank you, I had a large lunch." Grant could tell she was lying.

"Okay, I will get your order in right away." She nodded to Grant and then clipped his order to the ticket holder.

"So, how is work going?" Iris asked.

"It's fine. Nothing I can talk about, though, doctor-patient privilege and all." Grant said.

"Right. Of course."

"Hey, do you remember when we went dancing?" Grant asked. Iris looked a little confused.

"Sure." She lied. "What about it?" Grant showed her the picture.

"I like this photo; I was thinking about getting it framed. What do you think?" Iris's blue eyes flashed with anger for just a second, but then, almost as if she seemed to remember who she was pretending to be, she smiled at Grant.

"I think it's a wonderful photo of us." Just then, the waitress placed Grant's salad on the table. He poured the dressing on top and mixed it around a little, then tried a bite.

"Mmm. This salad is delicious. You should try it." He held out his fork with a small bite on it for Iris to try.

"Oh, no, thank you, I don't eat spicy things."

"It's not that spicy; come on, try it." He urged. Iris closed her eyes and leaned in to take a bite. When she opened her eyes, they were green. Grant looked around for a shadow or Verona herself but saw nothing, and when he looked back to Iris, she appeared to be as confused as he was. Iris tried not to show her confusion, but she looked nervous.

"Excuse me; I need to use the ladies' room." She said and got up from the table. She was gone for a few minutes, and when she returned, her eyes were blue once more.

"I never noticed how your eyes turn from blue to green; they're beautiful." Grant complimented. Iris smiled at him.

"I get them from my mother," She said. "You know, one thing I liked about you from the day we met is what a wonderful dancer you are." Grant sat down his fork and stood up from the table, extending his hand to Iris. Classical music played softly overhead, and there was a space in the middle of the room for dancing. *Iris is a beautiful dancer, but Verona always had two left feet.* Grant thought.

"You know, I'm suddenly not feeling so well. Could we just go back to your place and snuggle up on the couch? Maybe watch a movie?" Iris suggested.

"Sure, if that's what you want." Grant held up her coat for her, and she slid into it. He paid the bill and then remembered that he hadn't driven there.

"Do you have your car? I took an Uber here." He said.

"Yeah, I'm parked right there." Iris pointed to her car, a white Dodge Charger.

"Okay, I will meet you out there; I'm just going to use the bathroom before we go," Grant told her.

Grant didn't need to go; he needed an excuse to get away from Iris. He had forgotten why he had taken an Uber and had almost forgotten that he told Dunn and Adam they could stay at his house. He called Adam to let him know he and Iris were coming back. Grant told him about the guest house in the back and said they were welcome to stay there. When he knew that the coast would be clear, and Iris would not feel ambushed, Grant let her drive them back to his place.

Grant's house looked eerie from the road, the porch light was on, and a light fog obscured the driveway. The trees silhouetted the house and made it look like some haunted manor. The whole ride there, Grant had been thinking about how long he would have to keep this up. How long would it take to get that priest from Ohio? One thing was for sure, as long as he didn't anger Verona, he and Iris would be safe. Verona loved Grant and wanted to be with him, and having a living, breathing body to inhabit made that possible.

Grant and Iris went inside and got cozy on the couch. He brought blankets to the sofa and then changed into pajamas, just like the night he received the mystery call from Verona's phone number.

The movie had barely started when Grant felt Iris's hand reaching down into his boxers.

"Did you want to watch a movie at all?" Grant asked.

"Not really; it was just an excuse to get you alone." She turned her body to face him on the couch and looked into his eyes. For a moment, her face seemed to blur as Verona's facial structure pushed through. Grant jumped up, and Iris looked at him, alarmed. Her face was hers again, but her eyes were still as blue as the summer sky.

"What's wrong, Grant?" She demanded. "Don't you want this?"

"I'm just not feeling well right now. It must have been the chicken; sorry, I have to go to the bathroom." He ran down the hall and into the bathroom, locking the door behind him. Grant splashed water on his face. *Get your shit together!* He thought to himself.

Grant took out his phone and texted Adam.

Grant: Are you still here, in the guest house?

Adam: Yeah, what's up?

Grant: I can't do this, she is here, and her eyes, her face, she just morphs into Verona, and it's freaking me the hell out.

Adam: I'll be right there. I will knock on the door and make up some excuse to get you out of there. You can stay at my place tonight. Are you good to drive?

Grant: Yeah, I'm good. Thanks. I owe you big time.

Grant deleted the texts, just in case, and then went back to the theater room where Iris was sitting on the couch.

"You okay?" She asked.

"I feel a little better." He sat down beside her, and she leaned in to kiss him. Grant backed away and put his hand up to stop her.

"Sorry, I just threw up; probably not a good idea, you know, in case I'm contagious." Iris sighed and crossed her arms. She leaned back against Grant and begrudgingly began watching the movie.

A moment later, there was a pounding on the door. Grant went to open it and saw Dunn standing there. "Hey, sorry to bother you so late, but I need you. It's Adam." He said.

"What happened? Is he okay?"

"No, He's threatening to kill himself." Iris had stepped out of the theater room to see who was at the door. Grant looked back at her and shrugged.

"Sorry. I will make it up to you. Come on; we can take my car." Grant said, and Dunn followed him to the car. Grant noticed that Adam was laying in the back seat, covered with a blanket when he opened the door to get in. Adam held up a bottle of whiskey and grinned at Grant.

"You guys thought of everything, didn't you?" Grant asked. He pushed on the gas, leaving his haunted manor in the distance.

Adam's house was quiet, and best of all, there were no signs of vengeful spirits. Grant felt himself relax as soon as they were inside. Adam went to the hall closet and pulled out some extra blankets and pillows for Dunn and Grant. They opened the bottle of whiskey and tried to form a plan. Step one was: to find a priest to perform an exorcism.

If last week someone had told Grant that he would be entertaining the idea of possession, he would have laughed, and if someone had said Grant would be looking for an exorcist, he probably would have had them committed. Grant still wasn't entirely convinced that he wasn't crazy, but if he was, so were Adam and Dunn.

"What happened to your partner?" Grant asked. Dunn looked sad for a moment but tried to cover it before he spoke.

"She met some guy in Brazil and decided to stay. Sara got a job working at the U.S. Embassy, which is a huge step up from our department. It also means that they can take their time getting to know each other because she has a salary high enough to afford a place and has no need for naturalization to stay." Dunn said.

"Have you seen James?" Adam asked. "I never liked the guy, but I feel bad for him." Dunn shook his head.

"I feel bad for him too, he seemed like a nice enough guy, and it did seem like he wanted a future with Sara. He even bought them a house, a little place in the country. Now, it's nearly Christmas, and he will be spending it alone in the house he bought for them. I think he just moved too quickly for Sara, and it scared her."

Grant poured them all another glass. "Let's toast. To friendship." He said, lifting his glass to Adam and Dunn. They repeated the toast and drank their whiskey. They finished the bottle as they talked and took turns toasting. They fell asleep, or passed out might be more accurate. Adam curled up on the floor in a pile of blankets, Grant was sleeping on the couch, and Dunn was snoring in the recliner.

The morning sun lit the room, but it was the sound of Dunn's phone ringing that woke them. He got up from the recliner and took the call, pacing from the kitchen to the living room as he alternated between listening and speaking.

"That was the Priest. He started driving late last night, and because of low night-time traffic, he made good time. He will be here in an hour. We need to figure out where we are going to take Iris." Dunn looked at Adam and Grant.

"What about the old jail? You have that cell block that you hardly ever use because it's far away from the newly renovated section." Grant suggested.

"You're right. That would be perfect. I could get access, and no one else would even know we were there. Let's go. Father Murphy will call when he's close, and I will let him know where to meet us. Grant, You're going to have to go get Iris and bring her here." Dunn said with renewed vigor.

# CHAPTER THIRTY-FIVE

Adam and Dunn went to the jail to prepare a cell for the exorcism. The old jail was in the sub-basement that the department no longer used. When Dunn flipped the light switch, the old lights buzzed and flickered before finally lighting up the row, all except for one light at the end of the hall, which remained flickering like a strobe light in a haunted house.

Dunn unlocked the first cell as Adam wheeled in a laundry cart of items that they stockpiled. Dunn began digging through it and pulled out an antique set of iron ankle shackles.

"These will come in handy." The fold-down cot has steel legs that unfolded to support the weight of any size prisoner. Dunn wrapped the chain of the shackled around the legs of the bed so Iris would not be able to move much. He did the same thing at the head of the cot for Iris's arms. Dunn and Adam had brought down a mattress and put it on the cot.

"Well, the cell is prepared. Now we wait for Father Murphy's call." Dun began walking back toward the elevator.

"Cellular service is blocked down here, and we should head upstairs to wait."

Grant stopped by his office in the hospital, where he still saw patients from time to time. He had access to medical supplies, and he had seen more than a few mental patients become out of control very quickly when faced with treatment. If Iris was possessed, who knew what she might be capable of doing to them. Grant grabbed a couple of syringes and filled them with Midazolam, a fast-acting sedative.

Grant drove to Iris's house and was relieved that she was there and not at work. He hid the syringes in his pocket and knocked on the door.

"Hey, Iris, Want to go to lunch with me?" He asked when she opened the door.

"Sure, just let me grab my coat." She smiled at him before she turned away to collect her things. Grant noticed that her eyes were green. She was herself, Iris. Not Verona. Grant wondered if he had only imagined it and if they had to go through with this plan at all.

Grant drove them to a diner near the police department and got a table for two in the back, away from the windows. Grant's nervousness showed as they sat down.

"Is everything okay?" Iris asked.

"Huh? Yeah, sorry. Just a little distracted. Work was a little stressful this morning." *Could she tell he was lying?* Iris didn't seem to, but if she did, she did not call attention to it. They ordered and talked while they waited for their food. Grant kept looking at her as she happily talked about her job and whatever else crossed her mind, oblivious to what lay ahead.

Grant was ready to call the whole thing off, he was prepared to tell Dunn that they needed to wait and that he wasn't sure anymore, but then the headache started. Iris winced in pain and massaged her temples. She squeezed her eyes shut tight and groaned.

"Are you okay? Iris?" Grant put his hand on her shoulder, and when she finally looked up at him, his suspicions were confirmed in the pair of aquamarine eyes looking back at him.

"I'm better now. It was just a little headache. I get them some-times." Iris explained.

When their food got to the table, Grant ate quickly as Iris just moved the food around her plate; he felt his phone vibrate once in his pocket and knew it was time.

"I have to stop by and see Officer Dunn while we are close by; want to come with?" Grant asked. Iris agreed without hesita-tion, and Grant felt relief. This was the easy part, though. Grant didn't want to think about what he had to do next.

They entered the police department and headed for the ele-vator. Grant was thankful that no one else seemed to be needing it. His hand in his coat pocket wrapped around one of the syringes, and he could feel that his palm was clammy. As soon as they stepped inside the elevator, Grant pushed the button labeled B2, and their descent began. Before the doors opened, Grant took Iris by surprise and inserted the needle into her neck, emptying its contents into her veins.

"Grant, what are you..." She couldn't even finish her sentence before she collapsed into his arms. When the doors opened to the sub-basement, Adam and Dunn were waiting to take Iris to the cell. They strapped her onto the cot as Grant watched helplessly.

"You could wait upstairs if you want." Dunn watched as Grant wiped the tears away and sniffled.

"No, I need to see this for myself. I need to know that I have done the right thing." He thought of the oath he was bound to as a doctor. *Do No Harm*, he thought.

Father Murphy introduced himself and asked the three of them to join hands with him in a circle. He prayed for their protection, he prayed for their strength, and he prayed for Iris, the unwilling host.

"Let us begin." Father Murphy walked into the cell and began to read a passage from his Bible. Iris didn't move. Grant didn't take his eyes off her and was still not convinced that they were doing the right thing. He started to move toward the cell to stop the whole thing when the cot began to shake, and Iris began shaking violently. Grant heard her bones cracking and scraping as her back contorted in ways that he had never seen before. Dunn grabbed his arm and pulled Grant back as the priest began splashing Iris with holy water.

"Why does your spirit cling to this world? Cross over; your time is done." Father Murphy splashed Iris with the holy water again, and she sat up as far as she could and looked right at Grant. The look of betrayal on her face floored him, and he cried.

"What is your name? I command you, in the name of the father, the son, and the holy spirit, give us your name!" He splashed her with the holy water again, and she screamed out in pain. Iris turned to look at Father Murphy and spit at him. Iris's face seemed to melt away as Verona took her place. Adam stared in shock as he looked at his wife's face.

"Verona!" He shouted, and she turned her head abruptly to look at him. "Verona, I'm sorry that I wasn't a better husband; I'm sorry I didn't give you what you wanted." Verona's face seemed to soften as she tried to stand, to go to him, but when she realized her feet were shackled, rage took over again, and she slammed her body against the cot again and again with more strength than a woman her size should have. Grant watched in horror, unable to move or believe what he was seeing.

Verona called out to Grant. "Don't you want me anymore?" Her voice sounded innocent and sweet like she was trying to seduce him.

"Verona, You're dead. We can't be together. If you don't leave and cross over, you're going to kill Iris too." Grant pleaded. Grant mentioning Iris seemed to enrage Verona more, and she thrashed wildly. Instead of trying to escape, Verona banged her head- Iris's head- against the cot. Verona screamed in frustration at the mattress beneath her that softened her blows. Father Murphy began reading from his Bible again as Verona started to give up. She cried as she faded away, and Iris's face returned. The sedative was still working because Iris was perfectly still and peaceful.

"Let me look at her, please." Grant approached Iris and lifted her eyelid, revealing a beautiful blue eye. Her eyes sprang open, and Verona began to laugh.

"Did you think I could give up on you or us that easily?" She asked Grant. "Apparently, it was so easy for you to move on." She looked up at him, but it was Iris he saw. "Tell me you don't love me, and If I believe you, I'll go."

It wasn't Verona that Grant was seeing; it was Iris. He looked her in the eyes, her blue eyes. "I'm sorry. I don't love you."

Verona let out an ear-splitting scream. Everyone near the cell covered their ears. A bright light burst from Iris's body as her back arched and the cry intensified. A sinister-looking shadow rose from Iris. It was the shadow's sound, like the wail of a banshee on the wind. The shadow evaporated, and the cell was silent.

Iris lay sleeping, probably still under sedation. She looked peaceful. Grant hoped that she wouldn't remember what happened; he hoped that she would not remember that it was him, stabbing her with a needle in the elevator.

"How did you do it?" Adam asked Grant.

"How'd I do what?"

"Get her to believe you."

"I wasn't lying. I was looking at Iris. I love Verona with every part of me, but she's gone. Iris is here, and while I do like spending time with her, we are just getting to know each other. I would like to see what it develops into, but right now, I'm not sure it's love. I guess a half-truth was enough."

Dunn stared in disbelief. "Is it over?"

Father Murphy pressed his crucifix to Iris's head, and when he got no reaction, he turned to Dunn and nodded.

"What should we do with Iris?" Grant was expecting them to form a plan, but Dunn was already on top of it. He called an ambulance.

"Help me get her upstairs. When she wakes up, she will be in the hospital, and we can see how much she remembers." Dunn suggested.

"I'll stay with her," Grant said. "I hope that I won't be the last person she wants to see."

# CHAPTER THIRTY-SIX

Sara Jensen ran for her life through the narrow alleys of Complexo de Alemão as bullets pinged and sliced her surroundings. Angelo was ahead of her, pulling her by the arm, ducking this way and that way, through the twisted streets with no names or signs to mark them. She heard the dogs barking; they were hot on her trail. Angelo and Sara tried to run faster, but the dogs were relentless. One of them caught up to Sara and pounced on her back, knocking her to the ground. A shot rang out from above, and Sara opened her eyes just in time to see Angelo fall to the ground. His blood pooled around him, and then he glitched.

He disappeared momentarily, and when he reappeared, it wasn't Angelo at all but Kristofer. Sara heard Charlotte's blood-curdling scream, and she bolted upright. The lights were off in her bedroom, and she found herself drenched in sweat. Angelo sat up next to her.

"It's okay, Sara. It's just another nightmare. I'm right here." He draped his arm around her shoulder and pulled her back down into his arms. He held her until her heartbeat slowed to normal."

"Will the nightmares ever stop?" Sara didn't move. She took comfort in the safety of Angelo's embrace.

"I hope so. Just know that I will always be right here for you." Sara smiled and drifted off again, this time, into a dreamless sleep.

The next morning, Sara awakened to the smell of bacon frying. She got out of bed, pulled on a robe, and headed for the kitchen. The aroma of coffee brewing drew her in and dulled her senses to any other smell. Angelo prepared her breakfast and poured the coffee as Sara sat down.

"Are you going to the studio today?" Sara asked, taking a bite. The dining room was next to a row of Southern-facing windows; the view was spectacular, no matter the time of day. In the morning, you could watch the sunrise while you drank coffee in your robe, and at night, from the living room area just next to the dining room, you could watch the sunset while snuggling on the sofa to watch a movie.

Sara's job at the Embassy was just a security detail, but it paid a higher salary than she had ever seen in her lifetime. Angelo opened a dance studio with a loan from Julien and already had three classes filled.

Although Sara made enough money to pay the bills independently, she asked Angelo to move in with her. She felt safer with him around. Sara sometimes thought about James and the way she had left for Brazil and then just never returned. She had called him and ended things when she accepted the new job and it had not been easy. Sara was glad that she would never have to face him, but at the same time, she felt terrible about the whole situation. Sara took out her phone and called Dunn, she needed to hear a friendly voice.

"How are things, partner?" She asked.

"Well, You know that exorcism we watched in Brazil? It was unsuccessful. It was Verona's spirit that clung to Henry. We were finally able to get her to move on. Yesterday."

"How? Is Henry okay?"

"Her spirit was no longer possessing Henry; she moved on to Iris," Dunn explained.

"Who's Iris?"

"Dr. Hudson's new girlfriend."

"Oh, so she was clinging to Dr. Hudson; that's what was keeping her here?"

"Yeah. So how are you? Still having the nightmares?"

"I just can't seem to get them to stop. I keep replaying incidents in my mind, but the faces change. Like sometimes I see Kristofer dying all over again, then other times it's Angelo."

"It's fear. That's all. Have you thought about coming home? Maybe being in a familiar place would ease some of your fears?"

"I don't think I can. We are making a pretty good life here. I like my job, Angelo has his own dance studio, and we have a nice place in the city that I am buying. It's crazy. If someone told me even six months ago that I would be living in Brazil and working for the US Embassy, I would have laughed in their face."

"If anyone told me I would witness, not one, but two exorcisms and see the spirit of someone I knew to be dead, I probably would have referred them to Dr. Hudson."

Sara and Dunn both laughed.

"How's Charlotte?" Sara asked.

"She is great. She is still doing her private investigating. The department offered her a position as a consultant. We are officially dating too, so..."

"That's amazing! I always thought you two would be perfect for each other. I'm so happy for you!"

They talked for another twenty minutes before Dunn had to go. Sara felt better when she got off the phone. Happy that her friends were doing well and that at least her nightmares were only that, and nothing more.

# CHAPTER THIRTY-SEVEN

Grant sat by Iris's bedside as she slept. The exorcism took a toll on her body, and she had several bruises and a couple of broken bones. The doctors had to set a couple of them under anesthesia so that Iris wouldn't try to resist. It had been almost twenty-four hours since the exorcism took place, and Grant had not left her side.

Nurses came into the room periodically to take her vitals, check her IV, or just to check and see how Grant was doing. Grant didn't know what Dunn had told the doctors about her injuries or the sedation, but he knew that they could not admit to stealing sedatives, kidnapping, and witnessing an exorcism. Grant told them he knew nothing of how she came to be in the hospital.

Grant only knew because Dunn had called him, at least that was his story and the hospital staff seemed to buy it so they didn't press him further.

Grant took Iris's hand as she slept and held her fingers in his. Her hands were so smooth and soft. *I hope you don't hate me when you wake up*, he thought. Grant fell asleep in the chair beside Iris, her hand still in his. Sometime later, he woke to Dunn entering the room.

"How's she doing?" Dunn whispered.

"She's okay. She should be waking up soon, The doctor had to set a couple of her bones, and it would have been excruciating if she were awake. What did you tell them when they took her in?" Grant asked.

"I told them that we found her dumped in the alley behind the police department. I told them that this was how we found her and that we are investigating, so I couldn't say more."

"Smart," Grant told him.

"You wanna grab a cup of coffee or something? It looks like it would do you good."

"Sure. Cafeteria? I want to be here when she wakes up."

"Of course."

Dunn and Grant headed down to the cafeteria for coffee and breakfast. It took about fifteen minutes, but two nurses were taking her vitals when they returned to Iris's room, and she was awake. The nurses turned and stared at Grant.

"Wait out there, please." One of them said and closed the door to the room. Grant's heart started to pound in his chest. "Dunn, what if she remembers me jamming the needle in her neck? Worst of all, what if she remembers everything?" Grant started to panic.

"Calm down, we don't know anything yet, and what are they going to do, call the police? The department knows about this, I had to show them the tapes of Stacy levitating in her cell, and they got a full report of all that happened in Brazil. I got permission to use the cell in the sub-basement under two conditions, one, that there was a priest, and two, that there was a doctor on site. We had both of those things. Don't worry, the most that will happen is Iris will be angry with you." Dunn whispered so as not to be overheard.

"What about the drugs I stole to sedate her? What if they find out? The board would pull my medical license." He whispered back.

Just then, the door opened. "Okay, you can go in now." She said, and both of the nurses walked out. Grant breathed a sigh of relief. He rushed into the room and back to Iris's side. She looked relieved to see him but also confused.

"What's wrong?" Grant asked.

"How did I end up here with these injuries? The nurses were asking me, but I don't remember. The last thing I remember is you; you asked me to go to lunch with you. Then everything goes fuzzy." She said. Grant sighed and looked at Dunn. Grant knew he couldn't talk about it, not there.

"Let's just focus on getting you better right now." Grant rushed beside her and took her hand once more. She squeezed his hand. "I felt you here with me while I was asleep. I felt you holding my hand. Did you stay the whole time?" She asked.

Grant nodded. "I did. I wanted to be here when you woke up. How are you feeling? Can I get you anything?" He asked.

"No, I'm okay. I'm just glad you're here."

Dunn nodded to Grant and silently slipped from the room to give them space. He saw the nurse that had been in Iris's room walking down the hall toward him. As they passed each other in the hall, Dunn got an uneasy feeling that he couldn't quite identify. Dunn looked at her again, and her blue eyes seemed to stare holes into him, but she smiled and nodded in his direction. The feeling slipped away, the further he got from her. He let out a sigh of relief. *It's over, Dunn. She's gone*, he thought, reassuring himself. But he couldn't stop thinking about the nurse's eyes, those blue eyes.

## Acknowledgements

Firstly, I would like to thank my husband, Steven for being my biggest supporter. I dreamed of being an author my whole life and without his encouragement, patience, and savvy business skills, I would still be dreaming.

Thank you to my various writing groups on facebook and Tiktok, I have learned so much in the last few years about this whole process and I honestly could not have figured it all out on my own!

Thank you to all of my favorite authors, Stephen King, Anne Rice, Christopher Pike, RL Stine, Patrick Rothfuss, George RR Martin, Tolkien, and so many more that I am sure if I took the time to list them all we would be here, on this chapter for eternity. Thank you for telling your stories and letting me live in your worlds when I needed to escape my own!

Thank you to my Grandma, Charlotte, for passing on all of her Harlequin romance novels when she finished them. The first one made me blush and I reconsidered everything I thought I knew about her, I also learned that the horror and fantasy genres were more my style, and that was okay too!

As always, thank you. Yes, YOU! Thank you for letting me share my stories with you! I hope that my worlds help someone else like me escape their own reality for a little while.

Chey Carner is a graduate of the criminal justice program at Pickaway-Ross Career and Technology center. She also studied at Ohio University. She is a U.S. Army veteran, former teacher, and mother of two. Although she has a wandering spirit and has called many places home over the years, C.L. Carner, and her husband now reside in Texas with their two children, their golden retriever, a black cat named Salem, and a chihuahua named River.

Photo Credit: Christopher J Wurzbach